THE WOLVES OF FIREBORN PACK

FERAL INSTINCTS

USA TODAY BESTSELLING AUTHOR

GENEVIEVE JACK

Feral Instincts: The Wolves of Fireborn Pack Book 2

First EDITION: October 2023
eISBN: 978-1-940675-91-6
ISBN: 978-1-940675-99-2

V1.5

ABOUT THIS BOOK

A wolf denied can turn feral.

Of all the Fireborn pack royalty, werewolf Jason Flynn is the most virile, his raging appetite for the opposite sex well known among his pack mates. What they don't know is that his behavior is a salve for the wound he endured when his potential fated mate was murdered by a rogue pack member. When his playboy lifestyle becomes a risk to the pack, Jason resolves to change his ways—until a curse by an ex-lover sends his libido into overdrive.

Selene Andrews is an acolyte to Preotka Artemis, Fireborn pack's high priestess. Adopted as a homeless teen, she only desires to serve the pack as Artemis's successor. To advance, she must prove her mastery of the ritual magic required of a werewolf priestess. Opportunity strikes in unnervingly charming and seductive Jason.

When Selene is assigned to help Jason break his curse, neither of them understands the danger. Jason's beast is feral with instinctive hungers that threaten to consume celibate acolyte Selene. Curing him means working through Jason's tortured past. Only together can they truly heal, but can anything mend a broken vow?

CHAPTER
ONE

"You can't sleep on the bar, buddy."

Jason Flynn came awake to someone shoving his shoulder, his cheek pressed into the shiny wood surface of a bar that smelled vaguely of shoe polish. He lifted his head and wiped drool from the corner of his mouth under the judgmental scrutiny of a crusty and irritated bartender. "Sorry," he mumbled. But, in fact, he wasn't sorry at all. His impromptu nap was the best sleep he'd had in days. He held up his almost-empty scotch. "Another?"

"Maybe you should go home and sleep it off." The older man had an exceptionally long face with a handlebar mustache that Jason thought would've fit in perfectly at any saloon in the Wild West. All he was missing was a ten-gallon hat. "How 'bout I call you a cab?"

"Don't bother. I'll take him home," a female voice chimed in from behind him.

He squeezed his eyes shut against the surge of his wolf inside his body, a wolf that was starving for something Jason refused to feed him. Well, he'd tried to refuse him. In the months since they'd returned to Carlton City from Sable Creek, Wisconsin, he'd given in a few times. Compared to before Alex's attack, however, he'd been practically celibate... other than the days around the full moon when his wolf was in control. The part of his soul that was his inner beast protested the forced abstinence by restlessly twisting and pressing against the underside of his skin until he itched. He cast a disappointed glance at his empty scotch before slowly swiveling on his barstool to face his latest temptation.

A petite blonde with a Fireborn pack tattoo waited behind him with a flirty smile. "Hey, stranger!" She yanked him into a hug.

He made the mistake of inhaling as their bodies connected, and the scent of carnations, lilies, and rum filled his nose. His wolf whimpered, half-crazed within the cage of his flesh. He'd been with her before, although he couldn't immediately remember her name. The silky dress she wore skimmed every creamy curve. Damn, her body was a work of art. Refusing her might actually hurt.

"This isn't your usual haunt, is it?" She nudged his knee with her hip.

"No." This dive hadn't been on his radar until recently. The dusty hole-in-the-wall that smelled of spilled beer and forgotten dreams served mostly men who sat every other stool and stared at the bar or vacantly into their discount liquor in total silence. It was a great place to catch some z's. A horrible choice to pick up women. Which was the point. He'd come here to both numb his vice for sex and remove the temptation. "Yours either," he mumbled.

She laughed, and he couldn't tear his eyes away from her mouth. "I was coming from the club next door and noticed you in here all alone. I thought I'd better make sure you were okay." Her perfectly manicured nails brushed his thigh. "So... are you okay? Sounds like you need a ride."

While she spoke, he prodded his synapses, demanding they produce the woman's name. She was a pack member, an acquaintance, and someone he was sure he'd slept with on one or two occasions. Buying time by sliding his empty glass toward the bartender, he was relieved when his addled brain kicked out an image of a moon over a tree. Flashing a practiced smile, he said, "Luna Hawthorne, are you trying to pick me up?"

She tilted her head to the side. "Seems like it." Her gaze drifted over his wrinkled dress shirt and pants. "You look like you need a pick-me-up. Bad day?"

His jacket and tie were somewhere in the bar, collateral damage in the war he'd been waging with himself all night. Half-heartedly he ran a hand through his hair, then over the contours of his unshaven face, delivering a light laugh he didn't really feel. "Not sure what you mean. Couldn't be better."

Her smile waned, and she moved closer until her body was between his open knees and every man in the place was glancing in their direction with varying degrees of jealousy twinkling in their eyes. "Is it your vice?" she whispered. "Because, like, I can help you with that if you want?"

Every cell in his body ached, and his mind sent him some delicious porn-worthy images of what he could do to her in the bathrooms in the back, how good it would feel, how it would alleviate the pain. But he'd made himself a promise, and he wasn't ready to give up on it. Not yet.

"Not tonight, Luna."

She tucked her chin, then released a giggle. "Wait, what?" She looked confused. "You're turning me down? Have you found a mate or something?"

He shook his head. What he'd found was that his vice for sex had put his pack at risk. His last lover, Nickelova, had secretly been a dragon fae—a fairy who drew power from a bloodline that included dragon's blood. Unbeknownst to him, Nickie had been working with pack nemesis Alex Bloodright. Sleeping with her had allowed her an open door into their lives, access to his sister Laina and his alpha brother Silas. Once there, she'd magically circumvented all their defenses and manipulated them into a showdown with Alex, who'd challenged Silas for pack alpha. If Laina's mate hadn't had a fairy protector and been a dormant werewolf himself, the three of them would probably be dead. All because Jason couldn't keep it in his pants.

Afterward, Jason had sworn he'd give up his vice. His need for sex had become a liability, and he was unwilling to be a slave to it any longer. Only, his wolf wasn't on board with the plan and had made things like eating, sleeping, and simply existing without pain almost impossible.

"No mate." He bristled at the way her hand lifted to touch her chest, as if she was taking the rejection personally. "Believe me, I am tempted, Luna." He released a shaky breath. "Badly tempted."

Her brows knit, and those nails landed on his thighs again, giving them a little squeeze. "What's going on?"

"Nothing." He sliced his head to the right.

"Definitely not nothing." She laughed. "You turning down no-strings-attached sex is a reason to buy a fur-lined coffin because hell has definitely frozen over."

He bristled at that. It was true he had a certain reputation for being a playboy but only because his wolf needed the outlet to control the feral rage that bubbled just under the surface. The sex was a Band-Aid to keep from bleeding out and his wolf from doing something he'd regret. He didn't have that bandage right now, and his entire being felt like an open wound, one she was digging into without even knowing it.

"How long have we known each other, Luna?" Jason propped his elbow on the bar and leaned his head against his fist, exhaustion weighing on him like a lead coat.

"Two years."

"And we've... gotten together a few times before."

Luna bit her bottom lip. "Occasionally."

"And we're friends. Pack mates." His wolf was chuffing, adrenaline flowing through him at the possibility of having her.

"Yes, of course. Hello, you're the alpha's brother. You're a pack treasure."

Inside, he groaned. Just what he wanted, to be defined by his brother's accomplishments. If that wasn't a fist in the gut. But he didn't have the strength to show her any ire for the quip. Instead, he considered breaking his fast. She was safe. A pack mate. Something had changed though. When he thought about fucking her, he just felt... empty.

"How about this? Instead of us going back to your place, we go to dinner. Get to know each other." If she was his girlfriend, she wouldn't count as vice sex. Maybe that was the answer. Surely it would be easier to be monogamous than give up sex entirely.

"Like on a date?" She smirked, then shifted on her feet like the idea made her uncomfortable. "We... don't have *that* kind of relationship, Jason. I think it would be too confusing. People might get the wrong idea."

He pinched the bridge of his nose. Shit, thanks to his werewolf metabolism, he was starting to sober up, and he really needed the buzz right now. "What idea might that be?"

She snorted. "That you're interested in me as a potential mate. I used to think that was a possibility when I was younger. I'm sure you know I was smitten with you back when we were in school. After our first few times together, I understood it was about your wolf and our animal appetites. It's normal. I enjoy it as much as you do. But it will never be anything more."

He sat up straighter, rubbing circles in his palm with his thumb. "In the past, yes. But now I'm asking you on a date."

She sighed and glanced over her shoulder at the door. "I don't think it's a good idea."

He shook his head incredulously. "You're willing to have sex with me but not have dinner with me?"

She shrugged. "How will I ever find an actual mate if everyone thinks I'm being seriously courted by our alpha's brother?"

"I'm not claiming you, Luna, just suggesting we have dinner together." Why was she so resistant to this idea? Annoyance brewed in him, making his skin feel hot.

Backing up a step, she folded her arms. "I just... I need to have boundaries."

"Boundaries?" He raised his brow.

"After what happened to Jessica—"

"Don't." He shook his head. Jessica was his fated mate. Well, his potential fated mate. She'd been killed by Bloodright before Jason had a chance to claim her, and so the mating was never completed. Jessica's death was what kicked off his wolf's vice for sex. In some maladaptive hissy fit, his inner animal had decided the only thing that could fill the hole that Jessica left behind was sex.

"It was a tragedy, Jason. You suffered a deep trauma. It's understandable."

"This has nothing to do with her."

"But it does. We are not potentials. You'll never claim

me. If we dated, the relationship wouldn't have a chance."

"You don't know that."

"It's been two years. I think one of us would have felt the start of a bond by now if something was ever going to happen."

It was true. He didn't feel any sort of metaphysical connection to her. Not even a little bit.

"Sex with you, that's something else. I think of it as a service to the pack."

"Service to the— Being with me is *charity* sex to you?" With a pensive grunt, Jason stood from his stool, glancing around the bar for his jacket and finding it in a booth.

"I didn't say that." She spread her hands, looking frustrated. "How would *you* characterize our relationship? We haven't even seen each other in months."

He swiped his jacket and tie and set his jaw before he turned to face her. "Just two people who take solace from an unforgiving world in the safety of each other's arms."

Her laugh told him exactly what she thought of that description. "Perfect. Let's keep it that way then." Lips parting, she studied him for a moment, her hands landing on her hips. "What's this all about anyway? You've never been interested in dating before."

He sighed. There was one thing he could tell her that had nothing to do with the fact he was strung out from denying his vice. "My sister is getting married."

She paused, eyebrows creeping higher. "Oh my goddess, now this all makes sense. Laina's getting married. You don't want to attend your sister's royal wedding alone."

Flashing his most endearing smile, he walked toward her with swagger. "So… if dinner is out, do you want to attend a royal wedding?"

She shook her head. "I'm already going with Blade from Crescent City pack."

He groaned, completely defeated, and pulled his keys from his pocket.

She kissed him lightly on the cheek. "Are you sure you're okay to drive?"

"Yeah," he groused. "Later." He moved around her for the door.

"Jason?" He stopped short, darting a glance in her direction. "I can see you're going through something, and I hope you find whatever it is you're looking for."

He tipped his head in lieu of goodbye and shoved his way out the door.

TWO

The Bugatti Jason drove was capable of 260 miles per hour, but he crept along the winding drive that led to the gatehouse of his high-rise condominium at a glacier's pace. His mind was distracted with the evening's conversation. He'd vowed to quit his vice in the hospital when he'd been recovering from Alex's attack. What had happened with Nickelova had made him realize that he hated the life he'd been living. Hated the endless parade of women, the ones he knew from the pack and the humans he picked up at bars around town. He hated the smell of sex that clung to his skin. Hated the constant need to calm his inner beast.

It had been years since Jessica's death, and still he could barely think her name without stirring up a hurricane of emotions, which meant this thing, this vice that had its teeth in him, wasn't serving him, he was serving it. And while going cold turkey wasn't a ball of laughs, every day seemed to be getting easier. He was proud of himself for how he'd handled Luna even if the encounter had been a blow to his ego.

"A service to our pack," he mumbled grimly. He rubbed the back of his neck.

An Audi behind him honked impatiently. He waved his arm out the window, motioning for the driver to pass. As the car pulled around, he glimpsed the gray-blue hair of Mrs. Bloomburg. Great. Passed by an octogenarian. Her upturned middle finger goaded him from her window, her engine revving as she left him in her dust. And wasn't that just the icing on the cake to an otherwise disaster of an evening?

The road ended at a gatehouse where a slender redhead asked for his resident card. He held it out to her. Her fingers brushed his as she took it from his hand, and when he glanced up, she was staring at him intently.

"Have we met"—he read her badge—"Teresa?" He smiled in a practiced way, more out of habit than actual desire.

"No... I'm new." Her gaze traveled over his car and his suit before settling on his face. She sighed deeply.

"Really? Well, I knew there must be some explanation. I never forget a beautiful woman." He chided himself for flirting with her. He was playing with fire. He needed to stop. Right now.

The slight reddening of her cheeks made him weak. Scenting her, a rush of predatory energy flowed from his inner beast. He leaned out the window.

"Thank you." She handed his card back, her fingers grazing his again in the process and holding on. Heat sparked along his skin, and this time he was too tired to fight it.

"What time do you get off?" He managed to load the words *get off* with sexual energy.

"Four in the morning."

"Want to come up for an early-morning drink? I'm in the penthouse."

"Won't you be sleeping?"

He allowed a few of his wicked thoughts to leak into his grin. "Not if you come up."

Her cheeks pinked, her eyes darting to the corner of the small hut she was working in. "Maybe. I'll think about it."

Way to play it coy, Teresa.

"There's someone behind you," she said, gesturing with her head.

Jason checked his rearview mirror to find his neighbor raising his hands in frustration. "Hmm. We wouldn't want Mr. Anderson to dislodge the stick from his ass."

She gave a breathy laugh. "Have a nice night, Mr. Flynn."

He tipped his head in her general direction and continued to the parking lot. A short ride alone on the elevator and he arrived on the twenty-fifth floor of the Bachman Building, the best piece of real estate available in Carlton City.

He was already feeling guilty about the exchange by the time he opened the door. *Fuck.* Only one way to handle this. If Teresa did come up, he'd have to find the strength to turn her away. Or maybe not even open the door.

Inside, his penthouse apartment felt cold and lifeless, and he was reminded of why he'd spent his evening cozying up to a scotch. A human woman he'd met in New York decorated the place for him during their torrid affair. She'd insisted on it, tired as she was of staring at his bare white walls. The affair didn't last, but the decor did, and it was good enough to earn her a feature in *Architectural Digest*, a consolation prize, he supposed, for his failure to commit. She'd called it minimalist but welcoming: black stone, white oak floors, gray walls. There was an oatmeal-colored sofa that cost as much as a small village. He rarely sat on it.

He crossed to the fridge, the appliance perfectly masked to appear an extension of the cabinets, and hung his head inside. There was nothing worth eating, but he fished a half-full bottle of Sauvignon Blanc from the shelf and pulled out the cork. "Dinner is served."

Shedding his suit jacket, he took a seat at the designer table off his kitchen and flipped open his laptop. A few hours of work would clear his head. Sure enough, one of his scouts had a start-up he thought was worthy of Jason's attention—a tech company called Spackles with a patent for LED paint. It went on white but could change colors when connected to a power source. Jason clicked the link for background and financials.

Another email popped up, this one from Ryker Vandoren, an owner whose small business Jason had funded only a few months ago. Jason hadn't had high hopes for the project. It was a small occult shop in the vampire district, a niche market for sure and not in line with his usual investment profile. But Ryker had proved persuasive, supernaturally so, and before Jason could think too much about the opportunity, he'd already written the check.

He clicked on the email.

Jason,

Per our agreement, I've transferred to your account ten percent of my first quarter's net profits. See attached.

Ryker

Attached was a transaction confirmation in the six-figure range. Jason blinked, then logged into his account to double-check the amount. His eyebrows shot up. Perhaps Ryker's shop was a good investment after all.

His phone vibrated on the table. Laina.

"Rehearsal is tomorrow, Friday, seven o'clock. It will take several hours, so prepare yourself."

"Why hello, sister. It's good to speak with you. Of course I will attend your wedding rehearsal. I wouldn't miss it."

"Seriously, Jason. I'm not trying to be crass here, but I don't want your vice getting in the way this weekend. You can't be hitting on my bridesmaids or ushering the florist behind our cabin."

"I can go a day without having sex. I won't explode or anything." He was tempted to tell her he hadn't been with anyone in weeks but didn't want to jinx it. *Pride goeth before the fall.*

There was a long pause on the other end of the line.

"Are you still there?" Jason asked.

"Yeah... I know you can do it, but I need you sharp. Like I really need you and your wolf hypervigilant, understand?"

"Why? I'm not the one getting married."

Silence. He checked his phone to make sure it was still connected. "Silas was going to talk to you about this," she said finally.

"Spill it." Silas wasn't exactly chatty these days. If he had something to talk to Jason about, it was most certainly bad news.

"He put the word out about Alex and Nickelova to Soleil and the other celestial fae at Maison des Étoilles."

Maison des Étoilles was a bordello owned and run by celestial fae—fairies that drew their powers from heavenly bodies. The madam, Soleil, was an ex-girlfriend of Silas's. True to her name, Soleil's anchor of power was the sun, a boon for Silas as her presence could delay his need to shift. They'd broken up recently, but the two had remained friends, which was helpful to Jason's detective brother because the bordello tended to serve the underbelly of the city. The girls knew things and, lucky for Silas, were willing to talk.

"That's old news, sister. He asked her for help months ago. Last I heard, there'd been no sign of Nickelova or of Alex since you ripped through his abdomen. He's probably dead."

"There wasn't any sign. Until now." Her voice trembled on the other end of the line.

He nudged his laptop away to make room for his elbows, using one hand to massage the base of his aching skull. "What's happened?" He'd had enough of the anxiety roller coaster, but there was no getting off this ride, not until Alex and Nickelova were dead.

"Someone broke into the vault at Bojingles Fae Hospital and stole fire lily juice. There was nothing on any of the internal security recordings, but when the invisible thief was leaving the hospital, a device outside the entrance caught her moonlit reflection in the glass door to the building. A specialist on Silas's team blew it up and refined the image. It was Nickelova."

"Fire lily juice?" The juice of the fire lily could only be collected and administered by the fae, but it could cure a wide range of injuries and illnesses in supernatural beings. "She's still trying to heal Alex."

"That's what Silas thinks too," Laina said. "I nearly bit Alex's abdomen in two. He was bleeding out. I have no idea how she's kept him alive so long, but what else would she be doing with it?"

"Does Silas have any idea where she is now?"

"That's where Soleil comes in. One of her patrons was asking around about supernatural healers last night. Could be a coincidence, but..."

"It could be someone helping her," he finished.

"We all know if she is anywhere near Carlton City, she'll target my wedding. Pack security is on high alert. And if she succeeds in healing Alex, the entire pack is at risk."

He licked his lips. "I'll be there, and I'll make sure I'm ready for anything."

Once they said their goodbyes, Jason walked the periphery of his penthouse, ensuring every door and window was locked. Nickelova was one fish he hoped would get away for good. Far, far away. He hadn't known she was a fairy when he slept with her. Hell, he hadn't known her at all. They'd met at a bar, and he'd forgotten her first name almost immediately after they screwed. But she played him for a fool. She'd been helping the wolf responsible for the death of his parents and his potential mate. No doubt Alex still wanted to kill Silas and gain control of the Lycanthropic Society. Considering Nickelova had used Jason before for information and to lure Silas out of hiding, all three of them were potential targets.

Jason rubbed his chest, a wave of guilt dragging him under again. He should have been more careful. He should have known Nickelova was supernatural. His vice, his need for sex to calm his beast, had almost been his pack's undoing.

He finished off the bottle of wine, too antsy to work, and flopped onto his bed, the hour and the alcohol finally catching up to him. "A service to the pack," he mumbled as he drifted off. "The traumatized prince." Well, he couldn't argue with the trauma part. He fell asleep, fully clothed, the empty wine bottle still in his hand.

THREE

The blare of his phone's ringtone forced Jason's eyes open and he blinked rapidly against the lure of sleep. Four thirty a.m. Who the hell was calling him at this hour? His hand slapped clumsily at the phone, knocking the empty wine bottle he'd been sleeping with to the floor. It made a hollow sound as it rolled across the hardwood and clinked into the wall. Heavy with sleep, he fumbled with the device, desperate to stop the ringing. Somehow he managed to tap the screen and manipulate it close enough to his ear to be effective.

"Mr. Flynn? It's the night doorman. I have a Teresa in the lobby for you."

Teresa. Who the hell was Teresa? "Uh, who?"

"Redhead," the doorman whispered.

"Oh. From the gatehouse." He hesitated. "Send her up." He owed her a drink and an explanation.

Jason rolled out of bed and visited the bathroom. Considering he planned to send her away as soon as he could politely do so, he didn't stress over his appearance. He quickly combed his dark hair, swished some mouthwash to combat morning breath, and dripped Visine into his eyes to get the red out. Then he changed into a pair of sweats and a T-shirt. When the knock came, he was already at the door. She was still wearing her Bachman Building uniform, her smile taking up more than its share of real estate on her face. He invited her in and offered her a drink. One drink and then he'd explain and send her on her way.

"Wine," she said. "Whatever you have that's good."

"Make yourself at home." He drifted to the bar, leaving her standing awkwardly in the center of the room. He'd finished off the white, so he selected a bottle of red, Pinot Noir, and reached for the corkscrew.

"Do you live here full time?" Teresa asked, staring at the oatmeal couch, lips parted slightly.

He was surprised by the question. "Last time I checked. Why?"

She turned in a circle. "But, I mean, um, did you move in recently?"

Oh, she was commenting on the decor or lack of it. "Warm minimalism," he said. He finished pouring and crossed the room to hand her the glass.

"Huh?"

"The design. Clean lines. Simple decor. It's supposed to make you feel like you are the most important and interesting thing in the room."

Her lips twitched, a blush creeping from beneath her collar. Her gaze raked up his body. "I think it's working."

Fuck. Why did she have to look at him like that? He backed away from her toward the kitchen.

"Aren't you drinking?" she asked.

"I, uh, need to be honest about something." He gestured toward the sofa for her to sit. She glanced from her glass to the furniture, seemingly uncomfortable with drinking red wine on white upholstery. Eventually she sat down anyway, settling on the edge of the middle cushion.

"I never do this," she said through a smile. "I'm probably breaking some kind of rule coming up here."

"No one in this building will say a word to you. This is my fault." He perched on the arm of the sofa, calculating how far he needed to stay from her to keep his wolf at bay. This was a mistake. Inviting her up here was like an alcoholic inviting a bottle of whiskey for breakfast. His wolf wanted sex. It didn't matter who she was or what she looked like. The impulse was feral and intense enough this morning to make his hands tremble. And as much as he wanted to be polite, he needed to send her away, *pronto.* "I think you should go."

Understandably confused, she gave her head a firm shake. "What? I just got here."

He rubbed the bridge of his nose. "I know. I'm... I shouldn't have invited you up here. It's not a good time. I'm sorry."

Lips parting, she covered her eyes with one hand as if she didn't want him to see her cry. He hadn't meant to embarrass her.

"Teresa? Are you all right?" When she didn't respond, he tentatively rested a hand on her shoulder. "Teresa?"

After a beat, the woman lowered her hand, and all kinds of freaky hit the walls. Her eyes were *white*. Solid white and glowing like 60-watt incandescents.

"What the fuck?"

"Don't concern yourself, Jay, or should I call you Jason? It's so hard to know what's appropriate. You've had so many identities." An all-too-familiar voice came from Teresa's lips. He'd know that voice anywhere. Lowering his chin, he narrowed his eyes in disbelief.

"Nickelova?"

"Call me Nickie." Teresa's head rotated on her neck, back and around while the redhead's features changed, morphing into those of a sharp-featured woman with a sleek platinum bob. A wicked smile broke out across full red lips. "Miss me?"

Jason popped off the arm of the sofa and backed across the room. "What are you doing here?" The words came out in an anxious slur.

She stood, setting the glass of wine Teresa had been holding on the mantel. Then she strode toward him like she owned the place. When she was within reach, his hand shot out to grip her by the throat. "I should kill you after what you did."

"But you won't," she rasped through his tightening grip. "If you do, you'll be murdering the redhead whose body I'm possessing, not me."

With a grunt of disgust, he released her, not wanting

to damage Teresa. She didn't deserve this. "Coward. Where are you, Nickelova? Face me yourself."

She snorted. "We'll get to that."

"Why are you here?" he demanded.

"We had something, Jason. Don't deny it. You felt our connection. You feel it now." She winked at him, closing the space between them until she was close enough that he could feel her breath on his skin, smell her smoky raspberry mint scent.

"No, we didn't," he said, fighting his inner wolf with everything he had. The damned beast wanted control, wanted to touch her, and more. "I didn't even know who you were."

"But your wolf does. I can feel your beast even now trying to get to me. It's a fae thing. We're addictive to your kind, you know."

He shook his head. "Go, Nickelova. I don't want you here. Neither does my beast."

"That would be counterproductive. I need your help, Jason. Alex can no longer follow through on his end of our bargain. I need you to take his place."

"Fuck you and fuck off."

Scoffing, she paced the room, and he had the fleeting thought that she made warm minimalism look cold and deadly. "You don't mean that. You and I together? We'd be unstoppable. You can do what Alex can't. I need you, Jason. I want you to join me."

Goddess, the thought turned his stomach. "I said fuck off. The answer is no."

She folded her arms, her lips peeling back from her

teeth. "Just think about what we could accomplish together. The supernatural community has spent far too long denying who we are. With common leadership, a wolf and a dragon as king and queen, we could change everything. We wouldn't have to tiptoe around humans anymore. We'd be free."

"Do you hear how crazy you sound?" Jason snapped. "The supernatural communities have different traditions, different needs. They need different leaders. Plus it's the law of the goddess that we don't interfere with humans."

"That's how things are, but if we work together, it can be different. We can make it better. We can change the law."

"Never gonna happen," he growled.

Her eyes narrowed to slits. "I'm truly sorry you feel that way. I'd thought you might listen to reason, but if you want to be difficult." She raised her hands, forming a twisted square with her fingers. "Remember."

A grenade exploded inside his skull, light blinding him and rattling his teeth. The image of a map appeared in his mind, unraveling like a flag. There was a road, a river, and a space between two mountains. He didn't recognize the place, but a feeling accompanied the memory. A feeling that he could find the location if he tried.

"Come to me, Jason. I'll fulfill all your needs." Her eyes dropped to his crotch, and he felt filthy to have ever touched her. "Deny me and pay the price."

A growl ripped from Jason's throat. "You complete

psycho bitch from hell. Fuck off and get out of my house!"

She bared her teeth. "Oh, don't bother getting all high and mighty now, Jason. The deed's been done. When you were with me in Sable Creek, you signed a contract with your body. I cursed you, cowboy, and I'm here to activate that curse."

He cringed, heaviness overcoming him as if he had oil in his veins. He shook his head. "I didn't sign anything. I didn't even know who you were or what you were."

"Doesn't matter, Jason." She flashed an evil grin. "I gave you a little something to remember me by. You *will* remember and you *will* come to me. I curse you, Jason Flynn, and the wolf within you. From this day forward, your craving for sex will double every day you go without it. Every time you give in to your need, the act will bind you to me. It will give me power over you. I've planted how to find me in your brain. You can either come to me of your own free will or wait until your vice makes you my robot." She backed toward the fireplace. "Oh, and Jason, don't tell anyone about any of this, unless you want them dead." She snapped her fingers.

Jason felt a tug deep within his torso like someone had clawed open his chest and toyed with the deepest part of him. The fae bitch wasn't kidding. He could already feel the curse tainting him, making the vice he'd work so hard to get control of even worse than it was before. "Don't do this," he said through his teeth. "I swear to the goddess, I will kill you, Nickelova."

But Nickie was gone. The redhead was back, standing beside the fireplace, staring at her glass of wine as if she couldn't quite remember how she went from the couch to standing. She glanced at her drink, then grabbed her head. "I had the weirdest feeling just now."

"Oh?" Jason felt like a filthy creep for letting her believe it was all in her head, but telling her she'd just been possessed by a wicked fairy wasn't an option.

She frowned at her still full glass. "I think... I might have a migraine coming on. I should go."

His inner beast chuffed at the possibility of letting her go without fucking her, and Jason had to shove that side of him down once more. Thank the goddess, it wasn't close to the full moon, or he might not have been able to control himself. "I think that would be a good idea."

He showed her to the door. As he closed and locked it behind her, a soul-shaking fear rumbled from deep within him. Nickelova had used his vice to curse him. She'd laid the magic the first time he'd had sex with her. All she'd needed to do was trigger it. This was one STI that couldn't be cured with a shot of penicillin.

Disgusted, he staggered to the shower and turned the water on as hot as it would go. The soap wasn't strong enough, but it would have to do. He scrubbed in the scalding heat, enduring the self-inflicted punishment he deserved. His pack was at risk again, because of him, because of this hole he had in his fucking soul that he'd been trying to fill since Jessica was killed.

As the water flowed over his skin, he looked down his

body. His dick was hard as steel, and the throb of need inside him seemed to pound all the way to his temples. If he got himself off, would that bind him to her as well? Make the cravings worse? He turned the water as cold as it would go and stayed under until his teeth were chattering, relieved when his erection finally softened.

He needed help. But whom could he trust? If he told Silas about what happened, he could find himself in chains. The alpha might be his brother, but he was unforgiving when it came to Alex and threats to the pack. And with Laina's wedding coming up, his brother was already on edge. But if he told no one, Nickelova would use his vice to make him her slave. Because even as he struggled to wash all memories of her away, a tiny voice inside his head, one he knew was not his own, was already whispering about how much he'd enjoyed being with her before he knew who she was, and how incredible it would be to have her again.

FOUR

That night, Jason arrived in Red Grove feeling twitchy and uneasy. It didn't help that the tiny town was home to a cemetery that stretched on for miles, the army of headstones ending at the creepy Victorian home of demigoddess witch, Grateful Knight. No way did he want to run into her or her caretaker husband. The witch was a friend of Silas's, but Jason always found her eerily unsettling.

Per Laina's instructions, he turned down a winding road that led deep into the woods and parked near the quaint cabin by the lake where Kyle and Laina now lived. He could see why his sister wanted to get married here; the place was untarnished and magical. The early-spring blossoms on the trees above shed pink petals that swirled overhead and weighted the air with a floral scent that was decidedly feminine.

"Welcome. You must be Jason," a melodious voice said. He scented her before he saw her, his wolf nose detecting a luscious concoction of mango and vanilla with a hint of spice that cut through the other smells and drew his full attention. When he divined the source, he was not disappointed. She was tall, willowy, and dressed in a flowing pink robe that matched the blush of the petals that circled her perfectly coifed caramel-colored hair. Standing beside the twisting branches of an oak tree, she smiled at him, and the effect was like something out of a dream. Jason's wolf responded so fast and hard it froze him in place. He stared at her with an intensity he knew was inappropriate but was helpless to control.

Mine, his inner beast growled.

Jason gritted his teeth. This woman was certainly not *his.* He'd never even met her.

"Are you all right?" the woman asked, rushing forward to take his arm.

Her eyes were violet, a rare color he thought must actually be blue in the right light. But it was the innocence in those eyes and the soft, graceful way she touched his shoulder that unsettled him the most. His usually suave and practiced demeanor was nowhere to be found. He struggled to find his voice.

"I'm here for the rehearsal," Jason gritted out.

The woman nodded. "Of course you are." Removing one of the white flower leis that hung from the nook of her elbow, she looped it over his head. "I'm Selene. I'm an acolyte working with Artemis on your sister's wedding. I don't believe we've ever formally met."

"No," he said. He would have remembered meeting her. For forever and a day.

"I'm honored to help today. I'll show you back to where the others are waiting and where the ceremony will take place tomorrow.

"Am I late?" he asked.

"No. We're still waiting for the groom's brother to arrive."

Thank the goddess.

"Wait... Did you say you're an acolyte?" he asked. "You're pursuing the werewolf priesthood?" Jason's jaw tightened, and he realized too late that he was making a face like he'd smelled something bad. Inside, his wolf was still urging him to claim her. He had no idea if Nickelova's curse or his own attraction was to blame. That was reason enough not to act on his impulses, but this landed the last nail in the coffin of any interest he might have in her anyway. Acolytes were celibate, and they most certainly did not take mates.

Her eyebrows drew together at the look of disgust painted across his face. Before he could fix his expression, her gaze dropped to the forest floor. "If you'll follow me, the others are this way." She pointed a hand toward a trail leading into the trees. He followed her, walking side by side on the narrow path in silence. Fuck, he'd offended her. Goddess, he was a dick.

"I'm sorry for the reaction," Jason finally said. "That was rude of me. I haven't been myself today. This is all... harder than I expected." Skimming his gaze down her robes, his mouth went dry. He wanted to pull the bow at her waist and slip that robe off her shoulders. His dick twitched, and he redirected his attention toward a bird in the nearest tree.

"It's normal to feel some anxiety about your sister getting married. You may have feelings of pressure to marry yourself or fear that you'll never find a mate," she said in the rehearsed way of someone who was trained to counsel pack members. "Think of it like this: you're not losing a sister, you're gaining a brother," she continued. "The scrolls say that a wedding of any member of the pack is a reminder of our unity as a species. We're stronger when we work as one."

Her words hit him like a bucket of ice water. "The scrolls?" He laughed cynically.

She raised an eyebrow and laughed in a warm way that seemed to wrap around his heart and squeeze. "You're not a fan of our holy texts?"

"No offense, but I find it hard to believe that a goddess loved wolves so much that she turned twelve of them into men, only to curse them to return to their true form for three nights a month during the full moon. Oh, and while she was at it, further cursed them with individual vices that rule their lives almost as much as them turning into an animal once a month does." He laughed acerbically. "If there is truly a goddess, she's a bitch."

Selene balked, her jaw dropping. "The goddess didn't curse us!" Her eyes widened. "It was a blessing. She allowed us to retain an echo of our animal selves while inheriting a higher consciousness. Unlike our animal ancestors, werewolves have free will—we can choose. Our Primary ancestors were as close to wolves as humans have ever been and powerful enough to birth our entire race."

Jason snorted. Why were all the beautiful ones crazy? "Or a *Homo sapiens* got it on with a wolf and we evolved. Seems more likely."

"Why would that be more likely?"

Because I don't feel like a person with higher consciousness or free will, he thought. *I feel like an exhausted werewolf orphan who has to live a lie just to survive.* "I just don't believe the scrolls are anything more than stories. They're fiction."

Long, tapered fingers landed on Jason's forearm. The simple touch heated his blood, and he swallowed hard against the feeling. "The scrolls are so much more! People come to us all the time with their problems. Our sacred magic heals them when they can't figure things out on their own."

Jason tried to disguise his scowl. It was well known that the *Preotka* and her acolytes lived a lifestyle designed to enhance their spiritual connection with the next world. Even now, Selene's expression held not a flicker of cynicism or doubt. She looked at him like he was the only person on this earth and the purpose of her entire existence was to genuinely fix him if he needed it. *Fuck.* How could he ever accept her help, knowing that if he shared his vice, shared about the things he'd done with Nickelova and others, things he still wanted to do, he'd be ruining her innocence, tainting the very soul who so generously wanted to save him.

He grazed his bottom lip along his upper teeth and

was surprised when a bit of the truth snuck out. "I don't think what's broken inside me can be fixed."

"*Preotka* Artemis says that brokenness is the first step toward transformation. A caterpillar completely takes itself apart in order to become a butterfly."

"Gotta break a few eggs to make an omelet, eh?"

"She doesn't mean—"

He held up a hand. "Save your breath. My egg was fried on the sidewalk a long time ago. The only transformation happening here"—he placed a hand on his gut and winked—"is happening to the burger I had for lunch."

She pressed two fingers to her lips, covering a hint of a smile. They'd arrived at the clearing where Laina, Kyle, and Silas were waiting for him.

"Well, just think about it," Selene said. "It would be my pleasure to work with you. My door is always open."

As he watched Selene drift away, Jason wished he could take advantage of her open door, and not in the religious way. The thought confirmed he was a filthy predator. He sighed. Every moment with Selene would be like looking at his dark soul under a magnifying glass. She was pure, unadulterated virtue. A person like that could make anyone feel unworthy.

FIVE

Selene had never fully appreciated the rumors until now. Jason was strikingly handsome with a smile that stole the breath from her lungs. It wasn't every day a person got this close to a member of the royal family. Oh, she'd been in Jason's presence before at pack events and during the shift but always from across the room. They'd never been formally introduced. Royals didn't normally interact much with acolytes. Now she understood why people talked about him. Even in a business suit there was something potent about him. Her inner wolf had done an odd little twist when he'd looked at her, and she'd pictured, just for a second, what it would be like to have that mass of tightly coiled muscle stalk toward her in a dark room. But what had really surprised her was his charm and wit. Jason was someone she imagined she could talk to for hours. Although, as she watched him walk away, her spiritual side detected a darkness in his soul she wasn't expecting, a darkness she found more disturbing by the minute.

"What were you talking to Prince Jason about?" Artemis asked, her soft and straightforward smile giving her a younger appearance than her wrinkled skin and gray curls would suggest. She clasped her hands beneath the bell sleeves of her heavy purple robe.

"I sense something is troubling him, *Preotka*. He has a deep unease about him. I suggested it was common for a brother to feel anxious over a sibling's marriage, but his words seemed to indicate the problem goes deeper."

"And his aura?" Artemis was testing her. Aura reading was *Preotka* magic, something Selene was learning but hadn't fully mastered, like everything else in her chosen vocation.

"Muddy, with a green center. Much darker than it should be." She tangled her fingers together, nervous about the accuracy of her reading.

"I fear you are correct, sister."

"He's unhappy. But why?" Selene asked.

Artemis tipped her head. "Why do you think?"

Selene toyed with the end of her sash, twisting it around her finger. "I can't imagine. He has more wealth than most of the pack, a position of power, and if the rumors are to be believed, plenty of... social activity." Heat flushed her face and neck thinking about that. "Plus he has a loving family."

Artemis sighed. "He is wealthy but has no mate to share it with. He is a royal but not alpha. The women who keep his company are many, but none of them are here with him today. And the family you mentioned, they're all distracted with his sister's wedding. Too distracted to sense he's suffering."

Selene brushed a strand of hair back behind her ear. "So you think it's not just unhappiness but a sort of longing for more?"

Artemis shrugged. "We can't know for sure without asking the man himself. But I do know this. Years ago, Jason experienced a traumatic event that robbed him of his parents and his potential mate. That's when I first noticed the change in his aura and also when he began suffering from his vice for sex. I believe the two are connected."

Heaviness settled in Selene's chest, remembering the day Alex Bloodright murdered the Flynns along with other pack leaders and their families in a crowded theater. She hadn't known one of those people was a potential mate. Anyone would be traumatized after something like that. Was it any surprise that Jason had gone a little wild to ease the pain?

"Do you think we can help him?"

Artemis shrugged. "If and when he wants to be helped, we can help him. He's used sex to cope with the pain he's been feeling for a long time, and it's possible that works well enough for him. I suspect though that Silas will demand he find a mate soon. When that happens, he may want to change his habits."

"You've fixed vices before?"

She inclined her head. "Yes. But breaking a vice like this one could be tricky. He'd have to face the trauma he's distracting himself from." She straightened her sash. "In any event, this is all speculation. Jason might be perfectly content where he is in life, muddy aura and all."

Selene glanced over her shoulder at the group of royals gathered near the makeshift altar. Jason looked happy enough, laughing and joking with his family. Gerty and her husband Arthur, the king and queen of the woodland fae who called this forest home, had emerged from their trees and were mingling with the rest of the wedding party. Nate, the groom's brother, had also arrived. It was time to begin the rehearsal.

Quickly Selene said, "Artemis, what if I spoke to him, let him know we are willing to help? I mean if he does admit that he's unhappy, maybe there's more we can do."

"You have my permission to try, Selene. If you succeed, with help from the goddess, I will seriously consider it a sign you're fit for the next level on your spiritual journey." Artemis kissed her forehead and drifted toward the others.

A swell of pride filled Selene. The next phase of her spiritual journey was to advance to *Preotka*, to become priestess. It was the goal of every acolyte to be promoted to priestess and devote her life to serving the spiritual needs of the pack, but most acolytes never made it. Could she be one of the rare exceptions? A werewolf acolyte strong enough to win the goddess's favor and advance to the most respected role in the priesthood?

All that stood in her way of achieving the pinnacle of her life's work was Jason Flynn and his vice.

SIX

Jason checked his watch for the third time in fifteen minutes. He loved his sister, but the crawling sensation under his skin was only getting worse. After the incident with Nickelova, he'd gotten himself off twice, but the release proved superficial. His wolf was already begging for more, his need like a spring coiled too tight, ready to snap. He pumped his leg and wished Artemis would talk faster.

This was nothing like before. People called Jason a playboy, and he'd earned that moniker these past few years, but he'd never *had* to have sex. He'd gone weeks without it at a time with no physical symptoms. Emotional, sure. He'd remember Jessica and have to crawl into a bottle if he couldn't find another option. In that sense, sex was his vice. It was a balm for the pain that always lingered just under the surface. But this was different. Nickelova's curse had turned his need from a two on the dial to a twelve. He positively wanted to crawl out of his skin.

"Jason, I want you to carry the gifts for the goddess in the processional." Laina pointed at a prop platter with plastic fruit.

"Huh?" A bead of sweat narrowly missed his left eye, prompting a swipe of the back of his hand across his forehead.

"Silas is walking me down the aisle. I thought this would be a good way to involve you in the ceremony."

With a tight smile, he picked up the tray, blinking rapidly. "Of course. I... I'm happy to." Surely he could carry a platter of fruit? He licked his lips, his mouth as dry as the Sahara.

After a nod of appreciation in Jason's direction, *Preotka* Artemis began walking them through the ceremony from start to finish. She took extra time with Kyle and his brother Nate since their human upbringing meant they were unfamiliar with pack traditions. Twilight was upon them, the waning moon visible in the darkening sky. When Laina and Kyle were in position, practicing their vows, Gerty waved her wand in the air and sent a legion of fireflies to light up the space above their heads. Everyone oohed and aahed at the display.

Jason tried to appreciate the beauty around him, but he couldn't. His hands trembled beneath the tray of fake fruit. He was sweating in earnest now. At the first opportunity, he set the offering down and removed his jacket despite it being a cool spring night.

"What's the matter with you?" Silas whispered. "You're sweating like a sinner in church."

"I am a sinner in church."

Silas chuckled. "Seriously though."

Jason ran a finger along the inside of his collar. "Feeling a little under the weather."

His brother's bushy brow furrowed. "What kind of under the weather?"

"Like a bad flu." It wasn't a lie.

"Hang in there. This shouldn't take long. Afterward, you can see the healer so you're good to go tomorrow."

"Definitely." He planned to see someone about this curse, although he wouldn't call his friend a healer exactly.

"Can you alpha me into feeling better?" He gave his brother a tired laugh. "You know, take the edge off."

"That bad, eh?" Silas rubbed the stubble of his chin and contemplated his brother in silence. "I wish it were that easy. You can't alpha away the symptoms of illness. It only works on things under your control."

Jason swallowed down a wave of nausea. "Great."

Silas grimaced. "Damn, you really are sick. I think your face just turned green."

Jason rubbed the base of his skull. His headache pounded like a big bass drum.

"There is someone here who might be able to help," Silas whispered.

"Yeah?"

Silas pointed his chin toward the gray-haired woman reviewing the ceremony at the front of the aisle.

"Artemis?" Jason raised an eyebrow.

"She's not just a priestess in name. She and her followers have gifts from the goddess. A little of her voodoo is as good as any healer."

"I can't think of anything more humiliating than interrupting the priestess about this." Especially if she might suspect the real reason for his discomfort. Could Artemis see the curse upon his soul?

A burly palm slapped his shoulder and shook gently. "All right then. Guess you'll have to muscle through it."

With a deep breath, Jason glanced back toward Artemis, but it was the acolyte, Selene, standing behind her that commanded his attention. Dressed in that elegant blush-colored robe, she stared at him as if he were a puzzle she wished to solve. More accurately, she stared through him. Could she see it in him? Those violet eyes of hers seemed to cut right through to his soul. In the moment their eyes caught and held, it felt like someone was using a rib spreader to surgically open him up and fiddle with his heart. He gulped.

"Easy, buddy. If you're going to puke, do it over there." Silas pointed toward some bushes.

But Jason wasn't paying attention. He was picturing Selene naked and tied spread-eagle to his bed. He wondered if her sex was the same petal pink as her robe. No, Artemis couldn't help him with this curse, and neither could Selene. Hell, the way his wolf was eyeing her as his next meal, he'd be wise to stay as far away from her as possible.

WHY IS HE STARING AT ME? SELENE LOCKED EYES WITH JASON. The look on the man's face was that of a drowning man. Indeed, the intensity of his stare made her uncomfortable, stirred something deep inside her she hadn't known was there. Her heart rate increased, its thump steady in her ears, and a tingle started deep within her abdomen. Her wolf surged under her skin, wanting her to go to him. *Deep empathy,* she thought. A level of compassion she'd never achieved before. With a start, she recognized it must be the goddess calling her to help this man. The strong swelling in her chest and the magnetic pull she felt toward him was a sign from above.

But could she do it? Although she'd been trained to treat unwanted vices, she'd never put those skills to use before. Not because she didn't want to, of course. It was simply that an opportunity hadn't presented itself. There was one thing she had in common with Jason though, one thing that already connected them, the grief that came with the loss of both parents. That she could relate to, and if that was part of the cause of his affliction, she could help him.

As she watched him, she wondered if there wasn't more going on with him and his muddy aura. He looked ill. Obviously uncomfortable, he shifted from foot to foot. Even from a distance, his face appeared flushed and his hands trembled by his sides. Even Silas seemed genuinely concerned.

She told herself she'd speak with him after the ceremony. Helping Jason was her first priority, but she also felt an urgent need to prove to Artemis she was right for the priesthood. Silently she rehearsed what she'd say to him in her head.

"I believe that covers everything," Artemis announced from the altar in front of her. "I'll see you all back here tomorrow for the real thing."

As the wedding party departed in a throng of excited voices, Selene navigated the crowd toward Jason, hoping for the chance to convince him to work with her. But when she reached the place where he'd been standing with his brother, he was gone.

CHAPTER

SEVEN

Jason rushed from the wedding rehearsal feeling like he had a bad case of poison ivy. His skin itched and burned, and the throb at the base of his skull had grown more intense. *Boom, boom, boom.* The pain demanded attention.

The second he reached his car, he dug into his glove compartment and fished out a bottle of pain relievers, popping the cap and dry-swallowing three. The pounding took on a rhythm, morphing into a voice, Nickelova's voice. *Come to me. Come to me.* Her command echoed in his head until it became a stabbing sensation. He rubbed where it hurt the most. Jason had a nagging suspicion the discomfort was only going to get worse unless he found a way to break the curse. He needed help —magic powerful enough to undo what Nickelova had done to him. And he had an idea where he might find it.

Exiting the highway deep within Carlton City, Jason drove down the alley behind the Mill Wheel Night

45

Club, wishing he'd had the forethought to bring a gun loaded with wooden bullets. A couple making out behind a dumpster turned their heads long enough for the two puncture wounds on the woman's neck to gurgle blood that ran in lazy rivulets into her cleavage. Fuck, he hated vamps. If he wasn't desperate for a solution to his Nickelova problem, he'd never risk this part of town.

He parked under a rectangular tin sign that read RYKER'S LOST THINGS. The logo was a chipped etching of a boy in overalls with a bundle of his possessions wrapped in a kerchief, tied to a stick, and slung over his shoulder. An unsettling smile wrinkled his freckled nose. The sign squeaked on rusty hinges as it swung in the evening breeze.

Jason had loaned Ryker his start-up capital for this place, despite shady references and a business plan that was one step up from a cocktail napkin. Only Ryker proved persuasive, so persuasive that Jason caught on quickly that his aptitude for business wasn't quite human. And based on the return he'd seen come through his email, the guy had serious connections inside the world of the occult.

The bell over the door chimed, and the smell of dust hit Jason's nostrils. The inside of Lost Things looked like an episode of *Hoarders*. Stacks of books, artifacts, and shiny objects crowded the doorway. He had to turn sideways to slip between two large crates of Fabergé eggs, pausing halfway through when a low hum met his superhuman ears. It emanated from one large black egg that gleamed in the dim light, its ebony luster drawing him in. He leaned over for a better look.

"Don't touch that," came a smooth voice from deep within the shop. "Unless you'd like to spend the night locked inside that shiny trinket. I won't be able to get you out until sunrise. I need to move them into the back room. Haven't had a chance."

Jason stepped back from the eggs and made his way deeper into the dimly lit store. A squat woman waddled up to the counter with a handful of dried lizards. Her T-shirt read WITCHES DO IT IN CIRCLES.

"Do you sell these in bulk?" she asked the dark man behind the counter.

"Five for twenty."

The woman plopped down a bill. She waddled out the door, giving a wide clearance to the crate of eggs.

"Ryker Vandoren, how's my favorite client?" Jason spread his arms wide.

The man glanced up from his work and promptly disappeared, becoming a twist of smoke in a blink of an eye. The dark fog rolled over the counter and through the hodgepodge of collectibles. Ryker rematerialized near Jason, smelling of sulfur and dried things. Black eyes burned above a smile that boasted two overdeveloped cuspids. His olive-toned skin seemed to give off its own light in the haze of dust around them.

"Favorite client?" he asked. "Never try to charm an incubus, Mr. Flynn." His voice was pure silk and flowed from full lips like a whispered seduction. "It makes you seem insincere."

"Call me Jason. I assure you, I'd never attempt to charm you, Ryker. It would be like trying to sell an air conditioner to a polar bear."

Ryker blinked, a ghost of a smile turning the corners of his mouth. He narrowed his gaze on Jason. "What brings you here today? I've honored our agreement. Are you unhappy with your rate of return?"

"On the contrary, I'm impressed with your success. Who knew an antique shop for magical artifacts would do so well in the vampire district?" He rubbed the ache at the back of his head. "No, I'm not here about my investment."

The demon gestured toward the store. "Then what can I do for you?"

"I have a problem, and I think you might have a solution. But I need you to promise to keep this confidential."

Ryker's ears bent forward slightly. "We are alone. Your secrets are safe with me. I assure you, I have many."

"Well, yes. I assumed. That's why I came to you. I need your help. I have a problem with a dragon fae."

With a step back and a hiss, Ryker shook his finger. "Dragon fae are not my area of expertise. If you've offended the female, I suggest you apologize."

"How did you know I was talking about a female?"

"Because the only dragon fae to be in this city in a century is female."

"You've seen her?"

"No. But I've heard."

"I had a relationship with her."

"A physical relationship?"

Jason lowered his chin and gave an almost impercep-
tible nod. "And now she's haunting me."

The incubus's long, tapered fingers lifted to his
mouth to conceal a chuckle. "Even *I* wouldn't risk an
affair with that breed of fairy." Ryker's barbed tail
twitched behind him.

"For your information, I didn't know she was fae
when I was, er, drinking from her teacup. And now she's
possessing women I'm with and saying that every time I
have sex I'll trigger some kind of curse that will make me
her slave."

The demon whistled through his teeth.

"I need a way to break her curse."

Ryker took another deep breath and let it out slowly.
"The only way to break the curse of a dragon fae is to
remove her heart."

"As much as I'd like to do that, first I'd have to find
her, and then I'd have to have a plan for removing said
heart. That might take a while. In the meantime, you
must have a talisman or an enchanted gem that will
disconnect her from my... business?"

The laugh Ryker let out was gritty as though his
throat were lined with hot coals. "I am not a doctor or a
witch... or a witch doctor, for that matter." He quirked an
eyebrow. "I'm a demon, an incubus to be exact. I don't
know the nature of this fairy curse. Only another fae
would know for sure. But the fact that she possessed a
woman you were with and didn't simply pop into your
penthouse does tell us something."

"Like what?"

"Like there's probably a reason she can't come to you physically," he said. "She's cursed you to come to her because she can't come to you. That's likely why she used your vice." Ryker used a matter-of-fact tone when he mentioned Jason's vice, surprising him. "You didn't think I was aware of your vice? I feed off sexual energy, Jason. I smelled it on you the moment we met. Your reputation filled in the gaps. My presumption is this curse is attached to your vice."

"Just my vice?"

Ryker pointed at Jason's cell phone poking from his suit pocket. "From what I've been told, a dragon fae's curse can act like a computer virus. Every time you click on the link, it runs a program that accomplishes something nefarious in your device. Magic can attach to things, be introduced to a host in various ways. You are both man and beast, but your vice is the lowest common denominator between the two. The dragon fae left you a gift where it counts. Every time you get busy, she gets busy. A curse like that could be used to track your whereabouts, visit you through the body of your partner, influence your mind, even mess with your chemistry. All from the comfort of whatever hole she's hiding in."

"Mess with my chemistry?"

"Have you noticed your vice growing stronger? Harder to manage? You've got a monkey on your back for sex, my friend, and I'm willing to bet that monkey is about to get much heavier."

"That's what she told me. She made my vice worse, but if I indulge it, the curse will make me her puppet."

"Exactly."

"Fucking fantastic." Jason took a deep breath. "You need to help me. You have magical objects from every corner of the earth in here. There must be something that can extract a dragon fae curse."

He rubbed the smooth skin of his chin. There was a rumor that incubus demons were completely hairless aside from their eyebrows and the tops of their heads. Jason tried not to think too much about it or about how the man survived as an incubus.

"There is something...," Ryker said, eyes darting around the shop.

"Please."

"I have procured a demonic object with promising capabilities, but there is no record of a werewolf ever using it. Your kind is more human than my kind. There could be side effects."

"Tell me more."

Ryker coupled his hands behind his back and made his way through the stacks toward the office behind the counter. Once inside, he fished something out of a case on the desk.

"A long time ago, there was a demon who fell in love with a human. She wanted exclusivity. Silly. My kind is incapable of monogamy. But the desperate demon commissioned this ring from a witch." He held out a box with a carving of a serpent eating its own tail on the lid.

Jason flipped the box open, revealing a shiny platinum snake, body straight as a pin. "What does it do?"

"It mutates sexual desire into another form. For this

male, sex became hunger. It worked for a while. He took sexual nourishment only from his mate and filled his lust for others with food."

Jason reached for the box. "So then why is it here and not on some incubus living happily ever after?"

"The female left him. The demon, in his grief, refused to take off the ring. He ate himself to death. At least that's the rumor. I can't be responsible for verifying the stories of every treasure in this place."

"But if I wear this, I can avoid having sex. And if I avoid having sex, I avoid Nickelova."

"Nickelova! You *are* in deep. I was not aware it was the princess of the Siberian dragon fae who was gracing us with her presence."

Jason sighed. "How much for the ring?"

"You'd do better to visit a witch familiar with your kind. This might not be safe for you."

"How much?"

The demon considered him for a moment. "Forgiveness of my remaining debt to you should do it."

Jason did a quick calculation in his head. It wasn't much by his standards, and the royalties on his investment far exceeded the investment itself. "Only relief of debt. No change in ownership percentage."

Ryker bowed his head slightly in agreement.

"How do I use it?"

"Put it on your finger."

Instead of asking how he was supposed to wear a straight piece of jewelry like a ring, Jason poked the silver serpent. The snake came alive, inched over his knuckle, and coiled itself around his pointer finger. Immediately the dull ache he constantly carried between his legs eased. Or maybe it just changed into something else. A stomach rolling nausea moved in on its heels.

"I think it's working," he said.

"Good." Ryker narrowed his eyes at Jason, a cross between concern and self-preservation coming through his features. "As a precaution, don't leave it on all the time. Have you heard of Maison des Étoilles?"

Jason snorted. He knew Maison des Étoilles well. His brother, Silas, had dated the madam of the famed bordello. "I've heard of it."

"It's run by celestial fae. If there were a group as powerful as dragon fae, the celestial variety would be it. Not only are they resistant to another fae's possession, they have protections on the building that may prevent the activation of Nickelova's curse. Think of their magic as antivirus software." He pointed at Jason's phone again. "Go regularly. Take the ring off and feed your wolf."

"Thanks for the advice, but I'm done indulging this vice. Besides, I've never had to pay for sex before, and I don't intend to start now." He'd also rather not frequent a bordello run by his brother's ex—who still occasionally chatted with his big bro. The farther he could keep this problem from Silas and Laina, the better.

Ryker shook his head. "Jason, about this ring..." He trailed off as if considering whether to share more.

"What about it?"

"It's a temporary fix. It stores up all the wanting, all

the desire you feel while you wear it, and channels it into something else. But the moment you take it off, everything you were avoiding comes back exponentially stronger than before. Make sure you are in a safe place to vent your pent-up desires." Ryker handed him the wooden box the ring came in. "Also, keep it in this when you're not wearing it. Could be dangerous in the wrong hands. It's your responsibility now."

Jason accepted the box, a stiff sweat breaking out on his upper lip. "I think I need some air."

"Hmm." Ryker dissolved into a dark fog and blew through the store, re-forming at the entrance to hold the door open for Jason.

Feeling feverish and more than a little woozy, Jason made his way through the stacks to meet Ryker at the exit. He stumbled toward his Bugatti.

"Oh, and Jason..."

"Yeah?"

"Are you fucking crazy driving that thing in this neighborhood? Count yourself lucky you still have four wheels."

With a two-fingered salute, Jason slid behind the wheel and headed for home.

EIGHT

The ring was working. Jason had successfully avoided giving in to his vice and was still semi-functional, thanks to the silver serpent. Unlike the ring's previous owner, Jason's sex drive hadn't channeled itself into hunger either. On the contrary, he couldn't bring himself to eat a single thing, which wasn't much different from before the ring considering he hadn't had an appetite since the attack. Instead, the enchanted object had caused a perpetual state of lethargy and periods of fever as if he were fighting off a human illness. But after sleeping an unbelievable twelve hours and taking the maximum allowable dose of pain medication, he felt almost normal as he proceeded down the aisle at his sister's wedding as planned, the offering to the goddess balanced on his palms.

Alight with fireflies, the forest brimmed with dancing woodland fae who sang from the branches of their trees. Flower petals spiraled through the night sky over their heads, to the delight of the guests who sat in white folding chairs on either side of the aisle. Jason set the offering on the altar and took his position to the side, next to the other groomsmen.

Laina made a beautiful bride. Her off-the-shoulder gossamer gown seemed to float around her as she strode down the aisle. A canopy of bright green branches blossomed with glittering fairy magic above her head. And when she reached Kyle, it was clear the groom only had eyes for her. His hands wrapped around hers, entangled fingers a physical symbol of the sacred vows they were about to recite. How lucky she was. It was a goddamned miracle to be loved, really loved, and to give love back to someone in return.

Once the vows were exchanged, Laina detached the specially designed sleeve of Kyle's tux for the tattooing ritual. The biceps-triceps combo on the guy was as big as Jason's head. If he didn't know better, he'd swear Kyle had grown up a shifter and not a *dormant* as he had been until recently. Despite having only shifted a handful of times, Kyle's size and general appearance easily placed him in the more-than-human category.

Which made Jason even more aware of how less-than-werewolf he was at the moment. His normally muscular upper body had grown thin and wiry over the past few months. Not because of his vice per se, or even the enchanted ring he now wore, but because since Nick-elova eating was just a reminder of how alone he was in the world. He couldn't remember the last time he sat down to three squares in a day unless you counted copious amounts of alcohol as a meal. Nothing in his life had flavor anymore. Since the attack and realizing his lifestyle had played a part in it, he'd been caught in a spiral of sleepless nights and days filled with self-loathing, neither of which lent themselves to proper eating habits. And considering his increased metabolism —most wolves ate the equivalent of four humans— Jason's occasional cheeseburger was barely keeping him from starving to death.

He returned his focus to the altar as Artemis pressed the fang of Fireborn pack's Primary ancestor to Kyle's right shoulder, carving the tribal phoenix tattoo that denoted their pack. It was said the magic of the artifact caused the actual staining of the skin, but Jason always assumed it was a trick: ink stored inside the hollow of the massive tooth. With that symbol on his shoulder, he'd officially be one of them now, bound to protect and be protected by the pack. The *Preotka* shifted for a better angle, and Jason's gaze fell on Selene.

His mouth bent into a grimace. Everything about her vexed him. She was kind enough and beautiful... astonishingly beautiful. In any other scenario, if he hadn't been cursed, he'd have tried to get her into his bed. Only Selene was fine china. Aside from her celibate role as a religious acolyte for the pack, everything about her was pure and delicate. Untainted. He was afraid to speak to her for fear his words might pollute her ears. When she looked at him, he was sure she could see every grain of filth he hid behind his expensive clothes and brash atti-tude. And the thought of touching her... If there were anything good left inside him, he'd never sully her with direct contact.

Once again she was staring at him. Probably judging him. *Yep, all the pearl-clutching rumors are true.* With a sigh, he looked away, straight at the rows of guests. The witch, Grateful Knight, was in the second row with her husband, Rick, a young boy bouncing on his hip. That must be their son, Lucas. Cameron James was there too. Nice of him to come, given he'd been the one in the tux at the altar with Laina only a few months ago until Kyle had swooped in and interrupted what would have been a disaster of an arranged marriage.

Why was this taking so long? The familiar crawling feeling had begun again, like an army of ants rushing beneath his epidermis. He scratched his wrist. A breeze rustled the trees overhead, but he was melting inside his tux. Rocking onto his heels, he tugged at his collar.

Anxiously, he twisted the serpent ring on his finger and a wave of nausea came over him. Everyone was applauding. Why was everyone clapping? Oh, his sister. Artemis had announced the happy couple as officially married. Jason put his hands together in a delayed response.

A buzz started in his ears, growing loud enough to drown everything else out. At first it was white noise. Then the buzz took on a familiar rhythm, words he'd hoped had gone away came flooding back into his head. *Come to me. Come to me.* Nickelova's voice haunted him with every throb of his cranium. Louder and louder. It stabbed into his gray matter, constricting his vision.

Laina and Kyle walked down the aisle to whoops and howls of celebration. He was supposed to do something. Silas nudged his elbow, and he realized he was supposed to follow. He fell into step, working his way up the aisle between the chairs.

The voice grew louder and faster. *Come to me. Come to me.* Jason pitched forward, grabbing his head as a lightning strike cut through his brain. He moaned.

"What's wrong? Jason? Jason!" Silas was by his side, but there was nothing his brother could do. The horizon tilted and his cheek slapped the white cotton runner. A woman screamed. Silas bent over him, shook his shoulder.

But Jason couldn't respond. All he could see was Nickelova's face. All he could hear was her voice. *Come to me.* And all he could see was a road, a river, and a space between two mountains. This time he recognized the road. Route 9. And that was the Stone Eagle River winding under it. He could go to her. It would be easier if he'd go.

His eyes rolled back in his head and his back arched off the soft cloth runner, and then, mercifully, there was nothing.

Selene reached Jason's fallen body about the same time everyone else did. At the back of the impenetrable crowd, she craned her ear in his direction for any information on his condition.

"His vitals are normal," Grateful said. That's right, she'd been a nurse before becoming a witch. "There's nothing physically wrong with him. This is something magical, Silas."

There was a swoosh and the crowd parted slightly, giving Selene a view of the woman and her glowing purple sword. Grateful was no ordinary witch. She was a Hecate, a demigoddess charged with policing the supernatural. She lowered the tip of her weapon toward Jason's body and his skin *glowed*. Selene gasped.

"When Nightshade touches him, he lights up like a light bulb," Grateful said. "What the hell?" The tip of her sword glided down his arm, moving as if of its own volition. It stopped at his finger. Selene leaned forward to get a better look. The sword tip pointed at a serpent-shaped ring. With a short jab, Nightshade's tip connected with the object.

An ear-piercing shriek emanated from the jewelry. The silver dropped from Jason's skin and slithered away through the grass. Grateful raised her sword above her head and stabbed the silver serpent. Another screech and the worm disappeared in a puff of smoke.

"What was that thing?" Silas asked.

"Whatever it was, it was enchanted with very dark magic." Grateful returned to Jason's unconscious body, the sword glowing to life again. "It isn't just the ring, although I'm sensing it was aggravating his condition. There's something inside him. It's like... It's almost as if..."

"He's been cursed," Gerty said.

"Yes, cursed. I'm sensing fairy energy." Grateful shot a look toward Gerty. "Do you know who might have done this?"

"I do," Gerty said. "But perhaps it's a conversation best had in private." She glanced at Silas, Laina, and Kyle, the last of whom was rubbing his new wife's shoulders in a way that seemed to be the only thing propping her up.

There was a long pause, followed by frantic whispering. Selene strained to hear, but the voices drifted away on the spring breeze. Artemis stepped beside her, her lips pursing in concern.

"It appears you were correct about Prince Jason's aura," the older woman whispered. "There is more amiss than a simple vice."

She was interrupted when Silas spoke. "Let's move him somewhere safe. Somewhere we can assess him properly." The crowd parted and Silas hoisted Jason into his arms.

Laina placed a hand on her stomach, whispering something to Kyle over her shoulder. He nodded in agreement. "Bring him to the cabin. It's closest." There was an exchange of whispers between the royal family and the witch, and then all of them scattered.

Selene let out a deep breath and slumped her shoulders as the group disappeared into the woods, following the pathway back to the parking area.

Artemis cleared her throat. "It has been a long day, sister. I wonder if you might accompany the royal family and tend to their spiritual needs. I must rest."

"Yes," Selene said with enthusiasm. "I'd be happy to."

"Very well. Remember, the goddess is Jason's hope for recovery." Artemis handed her the box containing the Fireborn Primary Alpha artifacts, the same ones she'd used to bind Laina and Kyle just moments ago. Selene gazed at the sacred chest in wonder, honored to be trusted with it. Artemis gripped her shoulders, radiating confidence as if Selene might breathe it in. "Break this curse, sister, then see if you can help the man."

NINE

"Artemis sent me. I'm here to help." Selene ignored the slight shake of her knees and raised her chin in an effort to convey competence.

To her relief, Princess Laina allowed her inside the small cottage and led her to the bedroom where Jason had been laid out atop the bed's patchwork quilt. The crowd she'd seen before had thinned considerably, with only Silas, Laina, and Gerty surrounding Jason in the small room. It was clear the royal family wanted to handle Jason's condition discreetly.

"This is the work of dragon fae," Gerty said, smoothing her silver hair and lowering her chin to look at Silas over her bifocals. "Nickelova's magic, I'm sure of it. This type of fairy magic is rare and distinct. It's also, I fear, stronger than mine."

"Can you break the curse?" Silas asked.

Gerty approached Jason's body, drawing her wand. "Water, water, ever clear, take this blight and disappear."

A spray of thick fluid flowed over Jason, winding up and down his body like liquid mercury. His skin glowed red, and the spell went up in steam.

"It appears Nickelova expected my intervention." She sighed deeply.

"B-but you can try something else, right?" Laina placed a hand on Gerty's shoulder.

Gerty shook her head and tapped her wand against her palm.

"Let me try," Selene said. Every face turned in her direction.

Laina wrinkled her brow. "This is serious magic, Selene," she said, with an air of condescension that was unlike her. Selene supposed the stress was to blame. "It's going to take more than a few prayers to fix. Tell her, Silas."

Selene interrupted before Silas could say a word. "The artifacts of the Fireborn Primary were given to us by the goddess herself, along with the knowledge of how to use them. I've been trained for this."

"I thought that was all legend. Have you actually broken a curse before?" Silas asked.

Selene sighed, then reluctantly shook her head. "Well, no. Not in actual practice. But I've been trained for this."

Gerty gestured toward Jason. "She can't make this worse. If anything, it will give me a chance to think of what to try next."

"Grateful is researching an antidote in her grimoire," Silas said. "We could wait until she comes back."

"Who knows how long that will take?" Gerty stepped away from the bed, guiding Silas to the back of the room with a gentle hand. "Let the girl give it a shot."

Silas looked at her and nodded. "Fine. Do it."

Swallowing hard, Selene approached the bed. Anxiety made her mind go blank. She set the chest down on the mattress beside Jason and rehearsed the ritual in her mind. Taking a deep breath, she closed her eyes to steady her nerves. She'd never done this before—only learned about it in theory. And although she was sure she could execute the steps correctly, if it didn't work, she'd feel like a fool, like her entire life's work was a game.

"May I have a candle please?" she asked Laina. "Preferably white."

The princess left for a moment and returned with a thick white pillar but nothing to light it with.

"Allow me," Gerty said. With a flick of her silver wand, a flame sputtered to life. Selene nodded her thanks. Then she got down to business.

Leaning over the bed, she laid both hands on Jason's heart and began to chant in the original language of her people. The series of growls, grunts, and clicks combined with more human syllables was not used anymore, aside from her religious order and the orders of the other packs, but her song was an entreaty unto the goddess, begging for divine intervention.

Selene unbuttoned Jason's shirt as she sang, revealing his chest. The remnants of a broad, muscular physique lay wasted before her, wiry and sunken. He was emaciated by werewolf standards. Curling her lip, she thanked the goddess for her help revealing his affliction. Jason had been ill a long time.

With careful fingers, she uncorked a bottle of ink prepared with a single flake of the Primary's dried blood and dipped one of the Fireborn claws into it. Still chanting, she started beneath his navel, drawing a pattern of symbols in bright red, careful not to break the skin. The tribal prayer she designed stretched in a straight line, over his stomach, up his neck, to the center of his forehead. When it was complete, she wiped the claw clean on her own robes with a crisscross motion over her heart and returned it to the box.

The air felt thick to her now, and the candle's flame flickered more slowly, although she wondered if the perception was due to her deep meditative state and not a verifiable reality. Was everyone seeing things in slow motion? She retrieved the fang from the box, the same one used to carve the tattoo into Kyle's shoulder, and placed it on Jason's forehead where it shone white like a crescent moon.

Her song grew more urgent. The goddess must intervene. She called upon her from the deepest part of herself, from the purest depths of her heart. Carefully she removed the last artifact—a strip of the Primary's pelt— and draped it across Jason's chest.

Were her eyes deceiving her, or had Jason's skin taken on a purple glow? This was the part of the ritual when she was supposed to draw the curse from his body and welcome it into herself. Acolytes and priestesses kept themselves pure for a reason. A curse like this one would fizzle and die inside her, or so she'd been told. She passed her hands through the heavy air over his body, chanting and sweeping the purple energy toward her chest.

Rapidly, a longing stirred deep within her, an ache blooming low in her abdomen. What was this wanting? She leaned over Jason, her thoughts going places they'd never gone before. She could picture herself on top of him, riding him, grinding against him. Her cheeks grew hot. Sweat bloomed at her temples. A memory of her hand threading into his filled her mind. Only, the skin was much too pale to be hers. No, it wasn't hers at all. This was someone else's memory.

And then she saw something else in her mind: a road, a river, and a place between two mountains. *Come to me*, a woman's voice said. Blue eyes flashed from the face of a blond woman whose ghostly body hovered on the other side of the bed.

Selene ignored the apparition and leaned over to complete the ritual. She ended her song of supplication with a kiss to Jason's mouth. On contact, liquid flame coursed through her closed lips, down her throat, and into her lungs. She gasped, straightening and clutching her throat. The curse twisted inside her, worming through her torso. In her pain and panic, she couldn't remember the last part of the spell. Desperately she gasped for air, unable to free herself of the dark torment.

End how you began came Artemis's voice in her head. *Every prayer is a circle. Always end the way you began.*

Black spots danced in her vision. Frantically she turned to the candle and blew. Her breath came out black and ignited the flame as if she'd spit gasoline. Fire flared toward the ceiling. Hot, cleansing fire. Once the black breath was burned away, the flame extinguished, dowsing itself in a pool of melted wax.

Instantly she felt lighter, as if she'd removed a heavy weight from her soul. But the lightness turned into a spinning, floating sensation. She heard Gerty gasp. And then Selene's shoulder slapped the wood floor.

"What the fuck?" Jason sat up within a ring of gaping faces. Something dropped from his forehead, and he caught it in his hand. A giant fang. What the hell was all over him? He smeared the red symbols painted on his torso.

Laina and Silas were struggling beside the bed. Someone from the floor but Jason couldn't see who it was behind the full skirt of Laina's dress. His gaze darted to Gerty, whose wrinkled expression gave nothing away but was tight with concern.

"I'm all right," Selene's voice came from between them. The elegant blush-colored robe drifted into view as Silas and Laina parted. "Water please."

Gerty nodded and ran for the kitchen.

"What's *she* doing here?" Jason asked, bristling at the idea of the pious acolyte witnessing his embarrassing state. "Why is everyone staring? And why the hell am I in Laina's bed?"

Silas growled. "*She* just saved your life." His brother cradled Selene's elbow as she swayed on her feet.

While Jason tried to wrap his head around that tidbit, Laina stood and retrieved a towel from the bathroom, tossing it to him. He snatched it out of the air and started mopping his chest with it. Slowly the memory of what happened came back to him and he thumbed the base of his finger. "Where's my ring?"

"Grateful had to destroy it. It was killing you," Silas said. "Are you going to tell us why you were wearing it, or do I need to alpha the truth out of you?"

He scrubbed his face with his hands. "I didn't want this to happen. Not on Laina's special day. I was just trying to make it through the wedding."

Laina approached the bed and took his hand. "It's too late for all that. Just tell us what happened."

Jason darted a reserved glance toward Selene. "Can, uh, she leave the room before we talk about this?"

Selene tucked her hands inside her robes and looked down at her toes. "I already know, Jason. I saw it." Gerty returned with a glass of water, and Selene took a long drink before speaking again. "The blonde was trying to lure you somewhere. I saw a road, a river, and two mountains. I saw her beckoning me... I mean you. When the curse was inside me, I could see what you saw. She was luring you somewhere."

How did she know? He folded his arms, suddenly feeling more exposed and vulnerable than ever before.

"Nickelova?" Silas hissed through his teeth. "As we expected."

After a long, deep inhale, Jason admitted to himself that he could no longer keep his encounter a secret. "Yes. Nickelova." Goddess he hated this. "When I was with Nickelova in Sable creek, she attached a curse to my vice. I didn't know because it stayed dormant until a day ago when she possessed a woman I was with and activated it." He scrubbed his face with his hands. "If I don't... feed my wolf... my desire doubles. Each day it grows worse. If I do feed him, the curse binds me to her magically. Enough of that and eventually she'll control me. Either way, the only way to break the cycle is for me to go to her at the place she planted in my brain. And just so you know, she threatened all of you if I told. I'm only saying something now because of the circumstances." Circumstances being that he was outed by a nosey acolyte. He glanced again at Selene.

The others made a series of gasps and grunts.

"Goddess," Laina whispered. "How many times have you fed your wolf since Nickie activated the curse?"

"None," he said defensively. "That's what I was using the ring for. I have a friend who deals in enchanted objects. I was wearing it to help me... cope. Like I said, I just wanted to make it through the wedding, then I was going to tell you. I didn't realize the side effects would make me pass out."

Silas's hair was standing on end from running his hands through it, and Laina suddenly looked exhausted.

They'd all been through far too much tonight. Goddess he wished he could take it all away.

"So where is this place Selene mentioned? The river and the mountains." Laina spread her hands. "Maybe we should pay Nickelova a visit."

"I wouldn't do that," Gerty said, twirling her wand between her fingers. "Attacking a dragon fae in her mountain is like attacking a woodland fae in her tree. You'll never make it out alive."

"Even if we could, I have no idea where her mountain is. I recognize the road as Route 9, and it's Stone Eagle River, but there are no mountains in that area," Selene said.

"No mountains you can see," said Gerty. "Dragon fae can't make a mountain, but they can use magic to bend space. My guess is that if Jason follows her clues, she's left him a portal that will take him to her mountain, wherever that may be."

"I'll go," Silas said.

Gerty snorted. "Suicide. Do you think she'd let just anyone reach her? And if she did, do you believe for a second it wouldn't be a trap?"

"So Jason has to go," Laina said. "Or we have to lure her out."

Selene met the princess's gaze and wet her lips before speaking. "But... Jason can't go."

"What? Why?" Laina asked.

Jason squirmed as Selene's gaze shifted to him, cutting right through him.

"He won't be able to say no to her," Selene said. "You'll lose him."

Hungry and exhausted, Jason snapped, pointing a finger at the acolyte and barely suppressing a growl. "You don't even know me. You have no idea what I can and can't do. I would never put the pack at risk. I'd die first. How do you think I ended up in this situation? I literally almost died rather than give Nickelova more power."

Selene's chin dropped. "You *would* have died if it weren't for me," she said softly, eyes flicking up to his.

Goddess, he was such a dick. She'd saved him and he couldn't even bring himself to even say thank you. He desperately wanted her to leave.

Silas growled. "She's not the problem here, Jason. She's just trying to help."

Jason set his jaw. "If you want me to lead you to Nickelova, Silas, I'll go. I'm ready."

Silas's lips pressed into a flat line. "Why do you feel he can't do this, Selene?"

Jason tried to protest, but Silas cut him off with a look only an Alpha was capable of.

"When his curse was inside me, I saw what Jason saw and felt what Jason felt when Nickie... Nickelova cursed him. He wore that ring because he was desperate. His need is too strong without it. He won't be able to deny her."

"You don't know what you're talking about," Jason gritted out. He swung his legs over the side of the bed and stood, towering over Selene. She met his stare and stood her ground.

"What I did today returned Nickelova's curse to a dormant state," she began, speaking to him as if he were a small child. "But the seed of the curse remains attached to your vice. I couldn't remove it entirely because it's deeply imbedded in your wolf. To completely remove it, I'd have to take the vice too, and right now, that need is big enough the process would kill you. Which means, if you have sex, you could activate Nickelova's curse again." She tucked a strand of hair behind her ear and glanced at Silas before continuing. "Your aura is dark, Jason. You've fought your vice alone too long. Your soul is exhausted. If you continue as you have been, you will succumb to the darkness within and there will be no way for any of us to save you."

Jason's wolf raged inside his body, and he wanted to yell that she was wrong and no acolyte was going to tell him what to do. But those beautiful, pale eyes arrested him. How did you rage at someone who was graceful as the wind? It was like finding a kitten drinking your milk. Part of you wanted to swat it away, and another part wanted to give it a good cuddle.

"I can manage my own darkness, thank you very much," he said, the corner of his mouth turning up. "Maybe it's you who needs to make peace with your dark side. You seem a little obsessed with mine."

"Gerty, is there a way to lure a dragon fae from her mountain?" Silas asked, taking charge again.

"Hmm. Not exactly." Gerty cocked her head. "A

dragon fae's magic comes from her heart. It isn't a coincidence that she decided to help Alex. She loved him, which made her vulnerable. Whatever relationship she had with Jason, it was powerful enough for her to seek him out when she needed help. She may come for him again."

"And when she does? How do we stop her?" Laina asked.

Gerty's eyes landed on Jason. "When she comes for him, he needs to be ready to fight her."

EVERY PART OF SELENE'S BODY FELT HEAVY AS IF SOMEONE HAD injected liquid concrete into her bloodstream. She wavered slightly, slight enough that only Jason noticed. He was glaring at her, unblinking. Why did he hate her so much for trying to help him?

Silas placed his hands on his hips. "Gerty is right. Jason needs to be ready when Nickelova returns. We can't set a trap for her if he's going to cave to her seduction or be too weak physically to fight her."

"Hey, I'm not weak! And I'm not going to cave," Jason yelled. "I'm telling you, this... this girl doesn't know what she's talking about." He pointed a hand at Selene.

Laina smoothed the front of her wedding dress. "I think Selene's right. You need help. Nickelova took advantage of your vice before. We can't let her do it again."

"Says the woman who married her vice." Jason's face

reddened with anger. "It's been weeks since I indulged my wolf. I'm doing fine on my own."

"Then what was the ring for?" Laina countered.

He scrubbed his face with his palms. "I told you. The ring was to offset her curse."

Laina placed a hand on his shoulder. "You've done a great job, Jason. These past weeks had to have been hard. But you look like you haven't eaten in days. You passed out. You were barely breathing. Selene knows what she's talking about. You are too weak to face this alone."

He bared his teeth. "You're wrong."

Was that humiliation she saw in his eyes? Selene couldn't be a part of that. "I didn't mean to suggest he was weak, only that Nickie will trigger the curse again if given the chance," she blurted.

"I've heard enough." Silas puffed out his chest and went full alpha on Jason, who seemed to deflate slightly. "Gerty, do you think Nickelova knows Selene's broken her curse?"

The elderly fairy peered at him over the top of her glasses. "Probably not. The magic Selene used is rare and likely not on her radar. But she will know. The longer Jason stays away, the more she'll suspect something's gone wrong. If she hears he's reverted to his old ways but hasn't come to her, she'll know immediately. I highly recommend against that. The best course of action is to make Nickelova believe that he is still suffering under her curse for as long as possible."

Selene fisted her hands. "I can help you break your vice. With the help of the goddess, I can lead you through a program to end it and with it the curse that lingers there. If we destroy the vice, you'll be strong enough to face Nickelova when she comes for you. And she won't be able to reactivate it."

Jason growled. "I don't need your help. Frankly, you've done enough."

"What exactly does this program entail?" Silas asked.

"Daily meditation, prayer, diet, and the practice of ritual aura cleansing—"

"No way." Jason sneered at her like the mere thought disgusted him.

Laina huffed. "This is your life we're talking about! Selene is offering you a way out."

"Laina's right," Silas said. "Every day you are out there living your old life is a danger to the pack. Even if you abstain, she'll come for you again."

"I can beat this thing on my own," Jason promised.

"I know you won't ask for help," Silas said, his voice infuriatingly kind. "None of us are good at accepting assistance. Losing our parents has made us all independent as hell. So I'm going to make this easy on you. I won't make you ask. I'm just going to order it."

Jason's eyes darted between her and his brother. "What exactly does that mean?"

"I'm putting you in Selene's care, full time, until we get this thing figured out," Silas said.

"What?" Jason and Selene asked together.

Selene cleared her throat. "The program doesn't require my full-time care. I believe it can be accomplished with a half-day session three times a week."

Silas shook his head again. "It's too risky. We need someone monitoring him twenty-four seven, just in case she returns."

"Silas!" Jason pleaded. "What are you saying? You're assigning Selene as my babysitter?" He gaped at his brother in horror.

"More like your warden. She's proven herself more than capable of protecting you against Nickelova's magic. I want Selene to stay with you, full time, until your vice is completely cured and there's no chance of the curse activating again."

Selene cleared her throat, holding up two fingers to get the alpha's attention. "But I live in Sanctuary at Rivergate Manor. The *Preotka* won't allow it." Selene's heart raced. Surely Silas wasn't suggesting she actually *live* with Jason all day, every day. After all, the man looked as if he wanted to kill her at the moment.

"*Preotka* Artemis will be receptive to your assignment when she understands the safety of the pack is at risk." Silas clasped his hands together. "I assume Jason can't stay with you in Sanctuary."

"No." She chuckled softly. "Males are not allowed."

"Then you will stay with Jason at his penthouse until he's better. Do we all understand each other?" Silas looked between Selene and Jason.

Selene nodded, a knot of anxiety balling within her. If the alpha commanded it, she would do it. But no part of her felt ready for this level of solo responsibility and commitment. She swallowed down the fear lodged in her throat.

"You can't do this to me. I have work. I have a life." Jason bared his teeth and planted his hands on his hips.

"The faster you're cured, the faster you can have both of those things back," Silas said.

"You fucking bastard." Jason's wolf rose to the surface. Selene gasped as his eyes changed color and the hair along his arms lengthened. Without warning, he lunged and swung at Silas's head. Silas caught his fist, palm slapping knuckles loud enough to make Selene tense away from the crackle of testosterone in the room.

"Back down, brother, or things are going to get worse for you. Much, much worse."

Jason lowered his fist and wrestled his wolf into submission. He turned and paced the length of the room.

Silas never took his eyes off him as he said, "I'm going to step outside the door for a moment to call Artemis and make sure we're on the same page about Selene. I'll meet you out front and escort you back to your condo. Selene, take your time getting your things together. I'll wait with Jason until you can join us." He nodded his goodbye.

"I need to find Kyle," Laina said, hoisting up the skirt of her wedding dress and following after Silas.

Gerty gave one last empathetic glance toward Jason and said, "You can do this. I believe in you," before making her own exit.

Selene was left alone in the cottage with Jason. Although he didn't say a word, his gaze raked over her forehead, nose, and lips with barely contained revulsion.

She reached a trembling hand out and clasped Jason's fist, which had been clenched since he'd woken from her ritual. He jerked away from her touch, but she slowly and gently gripped his wrist and wrenched open his fingers. The Primary's fang rested in his grip. She slid the artifact from his palm and carefully returned it to the box, then gathered the pelt and folded it carefully, returning it to its place among the other artifacts, checking and double-checking that everything was where it belonged before closing and locking the sacred chest.

"You don't have to do this," Jason murmured. "You could refuse. My brother wouldn't deny you, especially if you asked Artemis to back you up."

"Why would I do that?" Selene shot him a glance. "You need me. I can help you."

Jason stepped in close, his body blocking the window and casting a dark shadow over her. "You don't want to live with me, Selene." His finger landed on her chest and traced the smear of blood that remained there from the ritual. "It's not safe. I'm a bad man with a vice. You're a woman. You wouldn't want to put yourself at risk, would you?"

Narrowing her eyes, Selene squared her shoulders, lifting the box from the bed in such a way that it banged into Jason's stomach. He took a step back with a resounding *oomph*.

"I don't believe for a second that you're capable of hurting me. And if you try, you should know I'm not as defenseless as I seem."

"Every woman has her vulnerabilities." His threatening tone made her spine tingle.

Exhausted from the ritual and in no mood to argue, she looked him dead in the eye and said, "Just remember, I saw into your soul. I know who you really are, Jason Flynn. Before you even think about messing with me, you'd better consider your own vulnerabilities."

CHAPTER
TEN

On the way back to his condominium, Jason had half a mind to drive directly to the security office of the Bachman Building and tell them that Silas, who trailed a car length behind him, was a stalker. He'd enjoy watching some half-trained, underpaid, overcaffeinated human in a blue uniform interrogate his big brother. Unfortunately, all it would take was a direct alpha command from Silas and life could get even worse... fast.

One word, said with the right inflection and eye contact, and Jason would be forced to obey or face the consequences—namely a body that burned as if he had acid in his veins. Rumors of alphas throughout history punishing their wolves by making them kneel on concrete until they bled or forcing them to take a hammer to their own hand were the stuff of nightmares. Silas had never done anything like that, but he was capable of it. Most people didn't realize it, but the guy had anger issues. Darkness lay beneath the buddy-cop exterior.

Silas would do anything to protect his pack, and that included torturing his little brother. Jason had no choice but to go along with this ridiculous plan. Or else.

It wasn't the program itself he was dreading. It was Selene. Giving up his vice for sex was difficult, both physically and mentally. It had been years since he'd gone this long without it. But Selene... Selene, with her perfect skin and her holier-than-thou attitude... Sweet, kind, virtuous Selene was a constant reminder of everything he wasn't. And now she was in charge. *Sesame Street* twenty-four hours a day.

He appreciated her saving his life. He did. And part of him regretted not thanking her for that particular service. But how creepy was it that she'd seen and felt the depravity going on inside his head? She'd likely never allow him to forget the filth he was. How he was dark to her light, tainted to her clean, unworthy to her admirable. And she'd be right there to watch him squirm as his vice tortured him from the inside out.

"Get out." Silas knocked on his driver's side window, looking peeved.

Jason turned off the ignition and climbed from the car. "How about a nice hospital stay? There's a rehab institute in Arizona where a popular pro golfer found some success."

"No. You need Selene. She understands the difference between a human addiction and a werewolf vice."

"And so do you, Silas." Jason tried to convey everything he was feeling to his brother in one dark look. "It's possible my wolf will go mad. That wasn't me who took a swing at you. That was a beast who's been denied too long, a beast who's been cursed and suppressed using dark magic."

Silas said nothing. They stepped into the elevator, and Silas pressed the button for the top floor: Jason's penthouse.

"Not her, Silas. There's got to be another way. I could... I could hurt her."

Wordlessly, Silas stepped off the elevator, waiting patiently for Jason to unlock his door.

"I was doing all right before Nickelova's curse. I'd gone weeks."

Silas closed the door behind them.

"Have you listened to a word I've said?" Jason stared at his brother in frustration.

Silas rubbed the base of his neck. "Want a drink before Selene gets here?"

Blowing out a deep breath, Jason nodded. "I'd love one." A crawling feeling had started under his skin, and his suit felt heavy and constricting. He removed his jacket and unbuttoned his top two buttons.

Although Jason kept a large variety of liquors stocked in the bar next to the fireplace, Silas went straight for the bourbon, pouring two glasses of Pappy Van Winkle. Jason didn't waste a second. He tossed the stuff back like it was lemonade and held his glass out for another. Silas obliged.

"Selene will be here soon. There's something I want to talk to you about."

"What?"

Silas made eye contact and held it. "You will not leave this apartment without Selene's permission."

It was an alpha command. The words sifted through Jason's cells and formed a heavy weight over his heart as his body processed the command. He snorted derisively. "You bastard."

"I didn't like the way you looked at her in the cabin. Almost like you hated her. You need her, Jason. Don't fuck this up by pushing her away."

"You don't know what you've done." Jason slammed the glass down on the counter.

"Jason—"

"I'm going to bed." He turned on his heel and headed for his room, leaving Silas standing by the bar.

GODDESS, HE WAS AN ASSHOLE. LOCKED IN HIS ROOM, JASON stared at the ceiling, the cruel ache of unfulfilled need gathering like a two-ton weight between his thighs. He'd heard Selene arrive and Silas leave, but instead of welcoming her or thanking her for saving his life, he'd stayed locked in his room, brooding over his predicament.

Why he'd thought he could sleep, he wasn't sure. His cock had an entirely different plan, and the long, thick length of him was currently pitching a tent in his covers. He stroked a hand over his sunken abs and palmed that sucker, stroking himself slowly from base to tip. It was a small reprieve, like a sip of air to a drowning man, but he'd suffered under his vice long enough to know the relief would be short-lived. Self-gratification tended to sate his inner beast for a short time, only to be followed by an increased desire for sex. It was like putting out the fire with gasoline.

As he arched his back and rolled his hips, pumping harder and faster, the build of pleasure felt like a roller coaster chugging toward that first major drop. He went over the edge, free-falling down the other side with a clear view of the broken track ahead.

And then *she* was there. It wasn't his hand but Nickelova's moving against him. He rolled onto his side and bounded from the bed, just barely making it to the bathroom before self-loathing turned his stomach. He heaved but there was nothing inside him to purge. When he was done, he checked his room, under the bed, in his closet. Thankfully, Nickie had been a figment of his imagination this time. Even the thought of her made everything feel tainted.

He turned on the shower and let the heat build. Stripping out of his pajamas, he stepped into the scalding water and scrubbed. His wolf was already revved up again, and as predicted, the edge of his need was sharper than before. He scrubbed harder, trading the need for pleasure for the sting of pain. Nickelova was on the edge of every orgasm, it seemed, curse or not. As he tipped his head back into the spray, he swore. He would not let her win. No fucking way.

Hours later, Jason lay on his floor, alternating sit-ups and push-ups in an effort to distract himself from his vice. Only problem was, he could smell Selene. Ripe mango and vanilla. She was right outside his door. There were other smells: food, breakfast he assumed. But his brain dismissed everything except the scent of the female. His inner wolf paced restlessly, eager to be in the presence of a woman. "Not this one," Jason said under his breath. "This one is seriously off-limits."

Unlocking the door, he passed through the short corridor into the great room, frowning when he saw a pallet of blankets on the floor next to the sofa. Beside it rested the ugliest brown plaid bag he'd ever seen. Was that her luggage? Had she slept on the floor last night? He clenched a fist against his stomach. Why hadn't Silas set her up in the guest room?

After a cursory check of the penthouse, he glimpsed her silhouette through the morning dew on the glass door to his balcony. Quietly he slipped outside. She'd exchanged her silk robe for jeans that bagged in all the wrong places and a T-shirt he found wholly unacceptable. Her complicated chignon was gone, replaced with a ponytail.

Legs crisscrossed on the concrete, her eyes were closed, her back straight, hands folded in her lap. He stepped around her. That couldn't be comfortable. It was cold out there, the spring chill hanging in the morning air. She should have a mat or, better yet, a chair under her.

"Why didn't you sleep in the guest room last night?" he said sharply. More sharply than he'd intended.

Her eyes opened, the sunrise constricting her pupils and turning her irises an intense shade of violet. He had to consciously stop himself from gasping. His lips parted, and he just took her in. A flock of black birds chose that moment to take off from the roof, their flapping wings and excited caws contradicting the weighty silence of her presence. Selene owned her space. The effect was intense.

"Good morning," she said, her soft smile belying her intense gaze. "I wasn't comfortable settling into your guest room without your permission. I'm here to help you, not to make myself at home."

Jason tried to respond, but the words stuck in his throat. He wiped a hand over his mouth and cleared the thickness from his vocal cords. "I... I can't have you sleeping on the floor. Come with me." Roughly he reached out and grabbed her by the arm, pulling her off the concrete and through the glass door. Aside from a guttural grunt, she didn't protest, though he suspected he was being too rough with her.

Moving like this, dragging her behind him like a child, kept him from thinking of her as a woman. He couldn't afford to look at her too closely or to consider the way her cotton T-shirt hugged her curves, not with his wolf pressing against his skin. Not with the crawling need that had kept him up all night.

He swept her ugly brown bag into the crook of his arm and lifted the pallet from the floor. He didn't stop until they were standing in his guest room. This room doubled as a library and was the one room in the house he'd decorated himself. Dark wood bookshelves lined the walls, overflowing with his favorite novels. A queen-size bed covered in a plush comforter in rich sapphire tones stood at the center of the room, bracketed by walnut end tables that matched a writing desk near the window. He tossed her things at the end of the bed. "Until I can convince Silas to end this, you'll stay in here. Understand?"

"Okay," she said, absently scanning the shelves.

"It would help if you told Silas you wanted to go."

That earned him her full attention. "But you need me."

He scanned her critically from head to toe and scoffed. "No, sweetheart. Look at you. This whole thing... It's way out of your league."

"Look at *me*?" Her brow puckered. "What's that supposed to mean?"

"You're not exactly dressed to sit at the adult table." He shoved his hands into his pockets and rocked back on his heels. "Come on. You're celibate. You know as well as I do you've bitten off more than you can chew with me. Do yourself a favor and ask to be removed from my case." He backed out the door.

"I'll do no such thing!" Selene protested, marching after him, back into the living room.

He stopped short when he saw the source of the breakfast smells and she almost rammed into his back. The kitchen counter was laden with pancakes, scrambled eggs, bacon, fresh coffee.

"I made you breakfast," Selene said from behind him. "It should still be hot."

He sighed. Most of the time the hollow feeling inside his abdomen was suppressed, hidden under the layers of constant wanting that drove his every decision. But now, seeing it all there, he almost felt hungry. "I don't usually eat breakfast."

"No kidding. Your refrigerator was a graveyard of half-empty take-out containers."

"Where did you even find the food?"

"I brought it with me. It's part of the regimen. You'll eat six times a day. Your body needs to be strong and healthy if we're going to beat this thing."

"Healthy." Jason's eyes drifted to the bar near the fire-place and widened when he found it empty. "What happened to the wine? The Macallan? The Pappy Bourbon?"

"Had to dump it," Selene said sadly. She shrugged. "Using it would interfere with our progress."

Jason's hands dug into his hair. "That was thousands of dollars of top shelf!"

Her laugh rang through the room like a bell, and he glared at her in horror.

"Relax, I didn't actually pour it down the drain," she

said. "Silas took it for safekeeping. You can have it back when you're better."

He dropped into a chair at the white oak table and rubbed his forehead. "So... the acolyte has a sense of humor. A cruel but existent sense of humor."

She crossed her right foot behind her left and bowed, her ponytail flopping over her shoulder. The movement made her look young and light like she was made of air rather than skin and bone. "We have a joke among acolytes."

He slouched. "Let's hear it."

"A werewolf, a vampire, and an acolyte walk into a bar. The bartender asks, 'What'll it be?' The werewolf orders a beer. The vampire orders a pint of blood. What does the acolyte order?"

"I don't know, what?"

"A candle to light for the souls of the vampire and the werewolf."

"That's the worst joke I've ever heard."

"Well, if we were comedians, we would have chosen a different vocation." She strode into the kitchen and started loading a plate.

"What is that in the eggs?"

"Onions, peppers, tomato, spinach. It helps with hormonal balance."

As she swayed in front of the counter, she added pancakes to the heaping pile forming on the plate in her hands. He shifted in his chair, his cock kicking. His inner wolf stretched and lowered his head, stalking her every movement. Breathing deeply, he sorted her mango and vanilla scent from the many others.

Selene didn't seem to notice his lascivious stare. She plopped the full plate in front of him and handed him a fork. "Please don't take this the wrong way, but I've noticed you've lost weight," she said. "Do you eat regularly?" Her voice was full of caring and concern, but all Jason's cock heard was a sultry murmur.

"Hmm?" He stared at the round curve of her hip.

She wandered back toward the food and started loading another plate. "Eating? Have you been... regularly?"

"Uh. I've been busy. Work and things. Plus I don't cook." His lids drooped as he followed the line of her body from thigh to shoulder to that long caramel-colored ponytail that swung behind her. He'd like to roll his hand in the length of it, tug her head back, and explore her mouth with his.

She cleared her throat. "Is something wrong?"

"Not at all."

"You are... um... staring at me." She plated her own food and walked to the table, taking the seat across from him.

"How could I not stare?" Jason flashed his practiced smile. "You're exquisite."

For a moment, she blinked at him, her body leaning closer as she studied his face and inhaled deeply through her nose. Then all at once she broke from his gaze and shook herself. "I'm also celibate, Jason. Your condition is going to make you see things that aren't there for a while. You might even see me as a potential target of your vice. But that's not who I am."

He swallowed a bite of breakfast, fixating on her full lips.

"Who are you then?" he asked.

"I'm the one who decides when you get to leave this apartment." There wasn't a hint of humor in her voice. Her back was ramrod straight and her jaw unflinching.

Under her unwavering gaze, Jason continued to eat, surprised how hungry he actually was. "What's in this? There's an aftertaste."

"It's an herb designed to support the healing process. The bitterness you taste is valerian root. It has a calming effect on your sympathetic nervous system."

"You're trying to drug me?"

"I'm trying to make it so you can sleep." She lowered her voice and turned her attention toward her food. "I heard you last night."

He swallowed the food in his mouth, mortified at the possibility she'd heard him pleasure himself. "What exactly did you hear?"

"You were showering in the middle of the night," she said matter-of-factly. "I presume the physical with-drawal symptoms were to blame. Racing pulse, sweating, crawling skin."

"I thought you said you'd never done this before?" In fact, he'd had all those symptoms at one point or another last night.

"Not with a vice like yours. I have never treated a

sexual vice, but I have studied alcohol addiction in were-wolves. There are similarities."

God she was beautiful, but she addressed him like a toddler. Was she judging him? Pitying him? The way she'd brushed off his advances was cold as ice, rigid, all kinds of palm up and no way. It made him horny as hell. Not only was she beautiful, she'd proved herself a worthy adversary. How he longed to tame her, bring her to her knees.

He took another bite, enjoying the fantasy that played out in his head. Selene on her knees. But even as he reveled in it, the vision warped from a sexual one to something else entirely. Selene on her knees in her ceremonial robes, praying to the goddess. *Fuck him.* She was an acolyte. What was he thinking, lusting after her? The guilt drove into him like a freight train.

"Once you're finished, we'll begin stage one," she said.

"What's stage one?"

Selene's violet stare cut straight to his soul. "I take you apart so I can put you back together."

ELEVEN

Selene hadn't meant her words to sound threatening, but from the way Jason's face paled and his fork hit his plate, they fell sharp and heavy on her target. What was she doing, saying it like that? Only, he'd shaken her to her core. That chiseled, almost gaunt face, the charming smile, the way his gaze raked over her... His words and actions promised delights she'd only dreamed about. She'd caught herself leaning toward him, thinking about how his lips might feel on her own. She'd smelled his desire for her, musk and spice, a heavenly scent that made her inner wolf far too interested. Thank the goddess she'd caught herself before things went too far.

"Take me apart?" Jason said. "What will that entail?"

The scent of desire was gone, replaced by the sharp tang of fear. Good. She pushed her fruit around her plate. "Attachments like yours don't develop overnight. This started with your wolf, true, but yours has morphed into a twenty-four-hours-a-day, seven-days-a-week addiction. For that to happen, there must have been a trigger —a cancer hiding in the dark recesses of your subconscious. Maybe you know what it is. Maybe you don't. My job is to isolate that trigger and bring it out into the light where we can address it directly." The truth was she suspected what the trigger had been. Everyone in the pack knew he'd lost his parents and his potential mate. But it wasn't about her knowing. It was about him admitting it, about giving him the tools to talk about it.

With a shake of his head, Jason growled low. "No. I don't need that. It's a wolf's vice, that's all. I'll break it, but I don't need you in my head to do it."

"No? So your need for sex exists only *before* the full moon, when your wolf is most active?"

He shifted, leaned back in his chair like a reticent toddler, and crossed his arms over his chest.

"You don't have to answer me. I know the truth. I saw it when I broke Nickelova's curse. This behavior, it's bled beyond your wolf, which means you're coping with something your human form is feeling." She sipped her coffee and waited for him to deny it. He didn't. "What we need to do is unravel exactly why this vice was able to get its hooks into you so deeply."

"So you're going to psychoanalyze me?" he gritted out. "What, do I lie on the couch and tell you how I lost my virginity?"

"I'm not a psychiatrist. I'm an acolyte for the priesthood. I don't want to tap into your mind. I want to tap into your soul."

If he'd been pale before, his current chalky corpse color redefined the term. He cleared his throat. "No."

She sat back, rubbing her palms on her thighs. "This is how it's done, Jason. I know you don't like me being here, but you want to get better, right?"

Jason's eyes tightened at the corners, seeming to size her up. "I'll need to do some work before we start. I have a few pressing emails I have to review."

"Can't it wait?"

"No. I'm an angel investor. People are counting on me."

She looked at him blankly.

"Our parents left us a large fortune when they died. My job is to use my portion of that inheritance to invest in businesses that need capital... after I vet them first."

"You just give them the money?"

"In exchange for a percentage of future profits. So, you see, as much as I'd like to dive right into your therapy, I have an obligation to my clients that comes first."

"How long will it take you?"

He stood and placed his plate in the sink. "A few hours. I'm sure you can, um, touch my soul later, right? Or tomorrow?"

She shook her head. "Jason—"

"Then it's settled."

Selene sighed heavily as he retreated into his bedroom, the click of the door locking behind him signaling the end of their conversation.

"TAP INTO MY GODDAMNED SOUL? OVER MY DEAD BODY." IF there was one good thing about Selene sharing her intended goals for the day, it was a temporary damper on his libido. He couldn't think of anything he desired less than to have Little Miss Virtuous poking around in his emotional attic. Jason plopped down at his desk and flipped open his laptop. He wasn't hiding anything per se, but it was the principle of the thing. Anyone with any sense of privacy would balk at the notion.

He opened his email and concentrated on reviewing the latest batch of financials from his scout, Andrew. He had a good feeling about this new company Spackles. He texted Andrew.

Set up a meeting with Spackles'
executive team

THE RETURN TEXT CAME BACK ALMOST
IMMEDIATELY.

Perfect. I had a feeling you'd see the
potential. How about Friday?

JASON LOOKED OVER HIS SHOULDER AT
THE DOOR.

Actually, I'm having a medical procedure.
Next week?

Is everything okay? Anything I should
know about?

Routine.

Thank God. We need you healthy. Baby needs a new pair of shoes.

JASON LAUGHED. OF COURSE ANDREW WANTED TO RUSH THIS ONE. HIS COMMISSION WOULD SET HIM UP FOR THE YEAR.

Next week.

I'm on it, boss. Take care.

Tossing his phone on the desk, he moved on to the next email, another company, another scout, another set of financials. What Selene didn't realize was, when it came to his business, there was always work to do. He could do this all day, all night if he had to. He supposed if he worked long enough, he'd prove to her he could break this vice on his own without the need for any religious mumbo jumbo.

Only, as the day wore on, Jason's vice had other things in mind. Although he stared at his computer screen, his wolf sent him a crystal-clear fantasy of hooking his fingers into the waistband of Selene's jeans, sliding them over her hips, and burying his face between her thighs. Mangoes and vanilla, that's what she smelled like. He wondered if the scent would be stronger or more defined between her legs. Would her skin taste sweet? Was her flesh as soft as it looked?

He got to his feet and paced the room. She said she was celibate, but she wouldn't be here if she wasn't curious. He could teach her to like it. *Fuck.* How could he be expected to maintain his distance with a woman who was in his apartment so willingly? He felt like a spider with a fly caught in his web, a fly he wasn't supposed to touch. Yeah, right.

He paced faster, a growl stirring in his chest. Silas should've known better than to send a woman. Of course, all werewolf priestesses *were* women, but that was just more of a reason he should have been allowed to face his demons on his own.

His dick was hard again and the need inside him was a fire demanding to be fed. Fuck, Ryker had warned him about the rebound effect of using the ring. His need was almost beyond his control.

Ryker..

Jason dug through the drawer of his nightstand. His hand fell on the box with the snake on the lid. He nudged the drawer closed with his hip and crossed to his desk. As far as he knew, Grateful had destroyed the ring, but that didn't mean Ryker wouldn't have a replacement. Turning the box over in his hand, he referred to the sticker with the Lost Things logo and phone number stuck to the bottom. He started to dial the number... but stopped with his finger hovering over the five.

Mango. He drew a deep breath in through his nose.

She'd walked past his room. His erection kicked and his wolf chuffed. A growl broke his lips.

Pocketing his phone, he glared at the door. It was too late for rings or potions. He needed sex, and he needed it now.

TWELVE

Selene squared her shoulders and screwed up her courage. Even though Jason was a royal, she couldn't allow him to push her around. She was here for a reason, and she was going to follow through with her commitment to Silas and to Artemis. The problem was, every time she looked at Jason—those piercing green eyes and that perfectly designed face—she experienced a wave of inappropriate attraction. Worse, her inner wolf was interested, chuffing and sniffing like she wanted to get closer to his beast. She was fairly sure the allure was an echo, left over from the ritual she'd performed. When she'd taken Nickelova's curse into her body, she'd had a taste of what it would be like to be with Jason, and she'd be lying to herself if she said it wasn't the single most pleasurable feeling she'd ever encountered in her work.

But she couldn't think about that. He'd never get better locked in his room. In fact, he'd missed lunch and dinner. His growing physical hunger might exacerbate his symptoms. And there was more at stake here than just helping him gain control of his vice. Her future as pack priestess was on the line. With a fortifying breath, she decided it was time for the two of them to start down his road to recovery.

"Jason?" She rapped on his door. "You need to come out now. Have something to eat. Begin your therapy."

Nothing.

"I'm becoming concerned. It's been over twelve hours since your last meal. I need to know you're okay in there." She knocked again.

Nothing.

"Jason, you're scaring me. I'm coming in." She tried the doorknob. Locked. Of course it was. The lever-style door handle was the type mainly designed for decoration. Not exactly tamper proof. She removed a bobby pin from her hair and stuck it in the tiny hole next to the lever. She heard a pop, and the handle gave way. But she'd barely had enough time to pull her hand away when the door flew open. She staggered back, dodging the swinging wood by mere inches.

From the belly of the dark room, Jason stalked toward her like a predator, chin tucked, shoulders mounded with tension. Yellow eyes tracked her every move. She barely recognized him. His presence had devolved to something purely feral.

"Jason, your eyes. Your wolf is too close to the surface." This shouldn't be happening. It wasn't even the full moon.

He inhaled deeply in response. Jason's skin gave off a

sweaty sheen, and his pupils were dilated. Selene wondered if he was fully sentient. And the smell, oh goddess, the scent of his arousal was a complex spice in the air that made her heart race and not just from fear.

She backed away, hands raised in the universal gesture for *stop*. A growl rumbled from deep within his chest, his longer legs chewing up the space between them. She scampered for the door like a fleeing rabbit. He couldn't leave without her permission. If she could get on the other side of the door, she could give him the space he needed while he wrestled himself under control.

She reached for the doorknob, managed to open it an inch. He pounced, shoving her against it, slamming it closed. She spun to face him, her backside bumping into the closed door. "Jason, stop!"

Pressing the full length of himself against her, his long, tapered fingers rose to wrap around her throat until his thumb stroked her pulse. "Let me out," he growled into her ear. Not his voice, more animal than human. The sound made her scalp tingle.

She couldn't speak through her fear-constricted throat, but she shook her head. No. She couldn't let him leave.

His knee pitched forward, wedging itself between her legs and thumping the door behind her. In this position, his thigh grazed her most sensitive flesh, his body heat covering her like the world's sexiest blanket. His weight pressed against her chest as he brought his lips to her ear again. "Let me out, now."

She attempted to push him away, but even with his diminished body weight, he was bigger than her, stronger than her. Her hands shoved ineffectively at his chest, the feel of his lean muscle against her palms awakening that thing within her she'd fought so hard to suppress. Why did he have to look the way he did? Against her wishes, her body responded, a rush of heat flooding her core.

He inhaled sharply. Damn, he could smell her excitement. He let go of her throat and caught her wrists in one hand, pressing them against the wall above her head. Was it possible for him to get any closer without being inside her? The thought made her insides quiver. His breath coiled against her lips.

All at once, everything changed. She was no longer an acolyte of twenty-five in Jason's apartment. She was fifteen, on a dirty mattress in the back of a truck stop, and a foul man was holding her wrists. The memory slammed into her, shaking her to her bones. Any desire she'd felt quickly turned to fear, and her breath came in ragged pants.

"Go!" she shouted. "I give you permission to leave."

Jason retracted immediately and snatched his keys from the small table in the foyer. She lunged out of his way as he barreled through the door.

Once he was gone, Selene pitched forward, catching herself on her denim-clad knees. The walls wavered, the air hot and oppressive. No. It wasn't the walls or the apartment. It was her. She was under attack from the inside. Panic. Anxiety.

She closed her eyes and thought of her anchor, that one supremely happy memory with the power to bring her back from the brink of a full-blown meltdown. It had been a long time since she'd needed to use it. But with her ghosts circling, the trauma of her past creeping into the present, she needed to employ the coping skills she thought she'd perfected long ago.

When she called on the memory, it was always the color blue she remembered first: a shade deeper than royal blue, but not quite navy. Edged in white, it was the color of a wall... no, a room. The blue room. Rivergate Manor. She was too dirty to be in that room, but the man who had brought her there had told her to wait. He'd seemed nice.

"Hello, dear." Artemis's gray spirals seemed to pick up a hint of the blue, further emphasizing the color of her eyes. Selene thought she looked like an angel. "My friend tells me he found you living under a bridge. Where is your family?"

Selene shook her head.

"My friend tells me he saw you shift last night."

Hugging herself, Selene's eyes widened.

"You didn't think I'd know about the shift? Oh yes. I'm a werewolf too. We all are wolves here." Artemis sat down on an upholstered bench near the fireplace. "Are your parents wolves?" she asked softly.

Selene shook her head.

"Did they kick you out of the house?"

How did she know? Selene looked down at her feet.

"It happens more than you might think. Lycanthropy

is genetic. On occasion, werewolves breed with humans and the gene is suppressed. It might rear its head two or three generations from the source. This can be terrifying to people unfamiliar with our kind."

"They're gone now. They moved," Selene said, remembering the day she'd come home from high school to find an empty house and no forwarding address. "I haven't seen them in almost a year."

"That's a long time to be living on the street. What are you... fifteen?"

"Sixteen. I'll be seventeen in January."

Artemis nodded. "How would you like this to be your new home? You can stay here with us and I'll take care of you. We'll become your pack."

Selene's eyes darted around the opulent room, from the gilded chandelier to the fireplace with its stone mantel. "Why... would you do that?"

Artemis smiled. "It's what the goddess wants. She sent you to us, and it is our duty to accept her gift."

"The goddess?" Selene laughed. She'd only known the god of her human parents.

Artemis took her hand. "Come, my child. Let's find you a room. There will be plenty of time to discuss all this when you're rested."

Selene emerged from the memory with a deep inhale, opening her eyes. She was a werewolf, an acolyte, a gift from the goddess. She was no victim.

"Oh no, Jason." If anything happened to him, Artemis would be so disappointed in her. He was her responsibility and obviously not in his right mind. She sprinted into his room, looking for anything that might give her a clue to where he might go.

Next to his laptop, a box carved out of ebony sat on top of a pile of paperwork. She'd seen the snake on the lid before. Yes, the ring Jason had worn. She flipped it open. Empty, of course. Still, Jason had been toying with the box. Why?

"Lost Things," she read off the label on the bottom. It was worth a try.

She reached for her phone. She was going to need transportation.

"Are you sure you want to be dropped off here, miss?" the Uber driver asked. "This is a bad neighborhood. Real bad. I won't be able to wait for you while you're inside."

Selene heard a high-pitched scream from somewhere down the alley followed by running footsteps that faded with distance. She hesitated. Stacks of books with worn titles waited just inside the front window, only one that she could read from her seat—*The Glory of the Dead.* An antique doll's head with a half-burned face leaned against the stack next to what looked like a human skull.

"I hate the sign," the driver said. "Look at the eyes. Is the little boy lost physically or lost in another way?" The big man shivered.

"I... I don't know," Selene said, glancing at the Lost Things logo.

"Well, it gives me the creeps. Either go in now or I'm

charging you for the ride back. I'm not staying here another minute."

She apologized and tipped him a few dollars. Steeling her resolve, she hopped out of the midsize sedan and hurried into the shop. The bell above the door chimed, heralding her entrance.

A man she was sure was a vampire turned from a shelf that held nothing but baskets of bones, sorted by size. He flashed her a little fang before resuming his shopping. The place stank of moldy parchment and bad taxidermy, but Selene shuffled deeper into the store.

"You're in the wrong place, angel." Another man had appeared out of thin air beside her, dark and menacing. Not dark-skinned, just dark. Black hair, black eyes, a complexion with olive undertones, and almond-shaped eyes she couldn't associate with any specific supernatural species or human ethnicity. His presence loomed as if the night air had become corporal beside her.

"I'm no angel," she said with more bravado than she felt.

"But your soul doesn't belong in this zip code." His voice was burning cinder blocks.

"I... Are you the owner of this store?" She held up the box.

He examined the item. "Interesting. Where did you get *that*, angel?"

"From Jason Fl—"

"Shhh. We have a strict privacy policy here. I know of whom you speak. What business is he of yours?"

"I'm supposed to be watching him... helping him. But

he went crazy and left his apartment. I need to find him." She lowered her voice. "He's not in his right mind. He might not be safe. Do you have any idea where he might have gone?"

The door chimed—the vampire leaving.

"I know where I told him to go, but it is no place for you, angel. Jason's vice needs to be fed, and with that dragon fae at large, there is only one safe place for him to do it."

"Where? Can I walk there from here?"

"Not if you want to arrive with a beating heart."

Known for her even temperament, Selene wasn't usually the type of person to act out. But she was tired and scared and woefully sick of the dark man's cryptic language. In one slick motion, she plucked a dagger off a nearby shelf and brought it to his throat, violently gripping the man's upper arm.

"Enough," she said with a growl. "Take me to Jason. Now! He's my responsibility. Whatever this place is, I can handle it."

The man dissolved from her grip. One minute there, the next a pillar of black smoke that smelled of sulfur. He returned to human form a few feet away from her. She lowered the blade.

He rubbed his shoulder where she'd gripped him. "No angel, indeed," he murmured. "Very well, I will take you, but I won't be responsible for the consequences."

THIRTEEN

Jason climbed the steps of Maison des Étoilles mechanically, awake but with arms and legs moving toward the bordello without any conscious effort. When he reached the door, it opened of its own volition. A slight figure with silky black hair and long pale limbs welcomed him inside. She was naked other than a grouping of starlike lights that hovered over her nipples and dripped like icicles down her abdomen and between her legs. Fae magic.

"Welcome." The smile the fae gave him sparkled unnaturally in the dim light.

"One," he said. He handed her a wad of cash.

She whispered something into a small microphone in a language Jason didn't understand. "Is there a name you'd prefer to be called?"

"No names."

She bowed slightly. "As you wish. Follow me." She led him deeper within the dark paneled walls and red velvet of the bordello. "We don't ask your desires here at Maison des Étoilles. Every girl is capable of reading your thoughts. She will adapt the session based on your deepest fantasies."

"How adaptable are they?"

"Within these walls, we can take on the form of anyone, man, woman, or beast. If you'd like multiples, one can become two, but any more require additional help. She'll ring me if she can't accommodate you." The hostess gave him a wink.

"One... woman is all I need. Thank you."

Opening a door for him, she fluttered her lashes in his direction. "As you wish. But please understand, our only goal is to please you. There's no need to hide anything from us here. We are rarely surprised by our guests' deepest desires." She turned and swayed down the hall toward the hostess stand.

He stepped into the room, the light from the hall extinguishing as the door closed behind him. For a moment, he was lost in darkness; then a red light clicked on, illuminating a four-poster bed with a gauzy white canopy. A curvy brunette slunk from the shadows, completely naked except for a black mask that covered most of her face.

"Look at those amber eyes. Someone is hungry," she said. "*Very* hungry. We won't waste another minute." She reached for his belt buckle.

He shoved her hands aside. He didn't want to be touched. All he was after was a fast, surgical coupling that would appease the wolf and give him control over his life again. It didn't matter what she looked like or what she said or did. That wasn't why he was here.

The wolf was in control as he spun her around and bent her over. It was instinct. Dominance. Action. He reached for his fly and was about to free his erection from its confines when she turned her head, looking at him over her shoulder. Her mask disappeared and the curvy brunette transformed into a long-waisted beauty with caramel tresses and violet eyes that flashed in his direction.

"Selene," he murmured. The change in her appearance did nothing to quell his desire. On the contrary, it ignited a yearning deep within him. No longer did he want a quick fuck. He wanted to touch her. Wanted to feel her silky skin. He reached out, his fingers coasting along the soft pale flesh of her back.

Her full lips parted in response, a moan spilling over that perfect pink tongue. She pressed her hips back, but he was still fully dressed, and he planned to stay that way. He couldn't, although he wanted to. Not Selene. Far from being a pleasurable experience, touching the Selene look-alike triggered shock waves that rolled through him like a ball of barbed wire. He could take her and it would satisfy his wolf's hunger, but it would also shred him. She was too good. Too pure. And he wasn't worthy. He rubbed at the heavy, sinking feeling in his chest. This was shame, pure and simple.

He staggered away from her.

The Selene look-alike reached for him. "My, my, Selene is a lucky girl."

"Don't do that. Don't say her name."

The woman stopped. "As you wish. Would you like me to be more aggressive? Your thoughts are conflicted."

Jason stared at her, torn between scratching his own skin off and taking her up on her offer. Fuck, he was screwed up. He pressed the heels of his palms into his eyes.

Unexpectedly, the decision was made for him. The door flew open and light as bright as the rising sun flooded over him. Soleil.

"Jason, what are you doing here?" His brother's ex-girlfriend entered the room, glowing like she'd swallowed the sun. And of course, in a way she had. Soleil, like all the women at the bordello, was celestial fae. Each had a planet or star that powered their existence. Hers was the sun itself, and the effect was extraordinary. "Do I need to call your brother?"

"No. And I'd appreciate you giving me the same privacy you provide your other patrons," he said, hands digging into his hair. He was ready to pull the damn stuff out.

"My other patrons don't have a werewolf acolyte sitting in my foyer demanding to see them, with an incubus demon backup no less. He's sniffing the customers, Jason. Some of my girls can feel him drawing on their energy."

"Selene is here?"

"Indeed." Soleil cast him a pitying look. "You and your money are welcome here, but not tonight. I'm sure you understand. The incubus is bad for business."

"I NEEDED A RELEASE. YOU SAW HOW DANGEROUS MY VICE CAN be, Selene. I might've hurt you if I hadn't used the bordello." Still could hurt her. His wolf, although distracted, had yet to be appeased.

Selene didn't say a word. She entered his apartment, looking tired and smelling slightly of sulfur.

"You shouldn't have gone to Lost Things. That place is dangerous. A woman like you could get hurt."

"A woman like me?"

"An acolyte. An innocent."

Selene tossed her purse on the sofa and retrieved a bottle of water from the fridge. "I'm not as helpless as you think."

"I don't think you're helpless, okay?" Jason took a seat at the table, feeling like a supreme asshole for everything that had happened that night. "I just think... what's going on with me is a little out of your experience level. I don't think this is going to work out. I need a different kind of therapy."

She strode toward him, leaning her hip against the side of the table, her round bottom coming tantalizingly close to the place his hand rested on the white oak top. Move his pinky an inch and he'd be touching her, feeling the firmness of her flesh taut beneath the fabric of her jeans.

"I'm here for a reason, and I don't give up easily," she said.

He heard her voice as if his head were underwater. He pictured his hand stroking down her stomach. A growl rumbled deep within him.

He licked his lips. His mouth had gone dry, bone dry. And her body shimmered like a cool glass of water. He squirmed under her violet stare, his gaze raking over her chest, her torso, her legs. Although it was clear she'd sensed him staring, she didn't move, didn't pull away. His wolf stood and his human body followed, rounding the table and pressing in close to her. His hands came to rest on either side of her hips.

"What are you doing?" she whispered.

"You're a beautiful woman. I know you're attracted to me. I can smell it."

"I'm here to help you. It's time to begin your therapy."

"Right. Tapping into my soul. Shouldn't we get to know each other first?" He licked his lips and lowered his face toward hers. Deep down, Jason knew he was crossing the line, but fuck if he could control himself. Her soft voice, the delicate bones of her face, everything about her was erotically female. And her innocence, that pinnacle of virtue he'd tried to avoid before, was a huge turn-on. She was untouched, an unclaimed land waiting for an explorer to plant his flag.

"Jason, this isn't..." She tried to slide out from between his arms. No way was his wolf going to go for that. His palm landed on her waist, her T-shirt bunching so that his hand touched a sliver of her skin. Heat scorched the narrow point of contact, electric sparks tingling through his arm and sending a wave of desire straight to his cock.

He lifted her bottom fully onto the table, positioning himself between her knees. She leaned away from him, her mouth working as if she wanted to say something but couldn't form the words. Bringing his nose close to her neck, he inhaled deeply. The sharp tang of her arousal was tempered ever so slightly by a whiff of fear.

"Don't fight it, Selene. It's natural. I'm a male. You're female. Just two people who need each other, taking solace from an unforgiving world in the safety of each other's arms."

"No," she said, but the word was flimsy and hollow.

"Hmm? Your words don't match the scent you're putting off, sweetheart."

"Don't call me sweetheart. My name is Selene." She patted herself on the chest between their bodies. "I'm Selene, Jason. This isn't you. It's your vice. Don't let it own you."

"What's your vice?" He sniffed up her neck to her ear, so close her body heat seared his flesh. "You're trembling. What is it that you can't get enough of?"

She stilled within his arms, serenity seizing her, filling her from the bottom up. Her violet gaze snapped to his, and the blush bled from her cheeks. "Helping people," she whispered. "I'm so sorry."

"Sorry for what?"

Selene's hands landed on his chest. He had a split second to notice the symbols painted on her palms, to wonder what they meant and how long they'd been there, before a shock rocked his body. His muscles seized as a hook seemed to slide between his ribs and dig into his heart. Unable to move anything but his eyes, his gaze locked on hers.

"I didn't want to have to do it this way. But you leave me no choice."

FOURTEEN

Selene's vision blurred, everything vibrating like a plucked chord. The walls melted away, and her spirit left her body, crossing into a dark place of spiderwebs and flashes of light. Pulses of energy flowed along strands that crisscrossed around her. Memories. Jason's memories. She was inside the core of Jason's personality, every experience tangled around her like a puzzle begging to be solved.

It was tempting to move toward the warmth coming from the light strands, but that wasn't why she was here. Oh, she'd do that eventually. Find his anchor the same way Artemis had found hers. But today she was searching for the source of his vice, a clue to the unfulfilled need that drove his addiction. She turned toward the darkness, the cold, a black tangle at the back of the web. Hidden deep within the shadows of his psyche, whatever it was made her shiver with dread. This was the source, the events that turned a simple, controllable desire for sex into an unmanageable monster that ruled Jason's life. If he were to overcome his vice, he needed to face this darkness. As she approached, a chill coursed over her skin.

Artemis and many others in the pack assumed his vice had started with the death of his potential mate, Jessica. He didn't like to talk about her, that was for sure. If it was about her, about grief and loss, he might have worked it out over time in years and years of therapy. But he didn't have years. Every day they were in this apartment was a day closer to Nickelova growing suspicious and coming for him. Whether he admitted it or not, he needed her. The faster he faced this darkness, the sooner he could walk fully in the light and the sooner he could free himself from Nickelova's hold over him.

Gently she reached out and touched the root of the darkest thread. For a heartbeat, it felt rough between her fingers, like spun asphalt, and then she was inside the memory, standing in a college classroom.

Most of the students were human, but she spotted Jason right away next to the only other shifter Selene could sense. At the front of the lecture hall, a female professor spoke. "Everything we take for granted comes from somewhere. It's a construct of our chemistry and our environment. What we consider sexual norms are simply those imposed on us by our community." Her eyes fell on Jason.

"Why is she staring at you like that?" the boy, the other shifter, whispered to Jason.

"None of your business."

"Is there something going on between you and Ms. Matthews?"

"Is there a reason you're not minding your own fucking business?" Jason's eyes darkened as he turned them on his friend.

The friend chuckled. "Dude, she's hot but she's twice your age."

"Still not your business."

The clock ticked to the hour. "Read chapter twenty for Thursday," Professor Matthews said. "Jason Flynn, I need to see you about your paper." She held up a stack of stapled assignments.

"Whatever." With a sharp look, the shifter next to Jason gathered his things and followed the others out the door.

Jason stood and descended the stairs of the emptying auditorium, Professor Matthews tapping the toe of her red pump as he neared. "I'm afraid your work isn't up to par," she said.

"I followed the rubric. Everything you asked for is there."

"Not everything."

"Tell me what's missing. I'll rewrite it."

"You know what's missing."

He swallowed, hard.

She gestured toward the door as a student entered early for the next class. "Come with me." She led him out of the lecture hall and across the building to her office. Jason's shoulders slumped, his expression like a lamb to slaughter.

Professor Matthews closed the door behind him, the lock clicking into place. "Now show me why I should reread this paper, Jason."

He dropped his backpack on a leather chair near the window, setting his cell phone on the seat next to it. "This has to stop."

"I'll decide when it stops. Do you want me to reread the paper, or will you be taking an F?"

Looking disgusted with himself, Jason snatched the paper from her hands and slapped it down on the desk. He grabbed her by the neck and bent her over until her nose touched the printed sheets. "No better time than the present," he said.

"Yes. Yes. From behind." Matthews purred.

"This is the last time," Jason said through his teeth. "It's over."

She cast him an evil grin. "It's over when I decide it is."

Selene wanted to look away from what happened next. It was obvious Jason didn't like Matthews, but he followed her instructions, did what his professor wanted him to do. She could feel his self-loathing, sense his disgust as he touched her. But she couldn't look away. She was experiencing this memory as if she were living it.

When the brutal coupling was done, Jason backed away like the very sight of the woman repulsed him. He zipped his pants and picked up his backpack, staring at the door while she composed herself.

"A-plus," she breathed, coming into his line of vision again and holding up the paper. "You're a natural."

Jason scowled, turning away. "Can I go?"

A number of missed messages flashed across the screen of Jason's phone from Silas. His brother had been trying to reach him. He clutched the phone near his chest as if the thing was an anchor, a talisman against what was happening in that room.

Ms. Matthews gripped Jason's lower jaw and forced him to look at her. "Such a pretty face. Don't feel guilty about this, darling. We're just two people taking solace from an unforgiving world in the safety of each other's arms."

"There's only one person here with anything at stake."

"Hey, you signed up for this. Do I need to remind you—?"

"No. I remember."

"Then I'll see you next... assignment." She unlocked the door and Jason bolted.

The scene faded, and so did Selene. She came out of his memories, exhausted and feeling filthy. She'd expected to experience the night Jason had learned of his parents' and Jessica's murder, but that wasn't his darkest moment after all. Instead, she'd witness a level of manipulation and abuse that made bile rise in her throat.

Once she'd collected herself, it took her a moment to realize she was still perched on the table with Jason awake but unresponsive between her thighs. Promptly she removed her hands from his chest to halt the ritual.

And watched him collapse on the floor near her feet.

Jason hit the floor and rolled onto his back. Everything hurt as if Selene had reached down his throat, grabbed his intestines, and wrapped them around the bumper of a moving bus. He curled on his side and heaved. There was nothing inside him to come out. Truly nothing. He felt like an empty husk.

"Just lie still," Selene said softly. "You'll be all right. You just need rest."

He couldn't have responded if he'd wanted to. His body shivered uncontrollably, his teeth chattering. Every sweat gland seemed to open at once, quickly soaking through the front of his shirt.

She pressed two fingers against his neck and frowned. "Let's get you into bed."

Hooking her hands under his armpits, she dragged him into the bedroom and lifted him onto the mattress, a feat that wouldn't have been possible had she not been a werewolf. His muscles were useless, twitching things. He couldn't help her or fight her.

She unbuttoned his wet shirt and rolled him out of it. There was nothing sexual about the act. If anything, it was humiliating, although he was too tired to register that particular emotion. He blinked, and she was gone.

When he opened his eyes again, Selene was wringing a washcloth in a basin. She lifted one of his arms and scrubbed. She rinsed it out again. Jason closed his eyes.

He opened them again, and he was in his pajamas. She was there, sitting by his bed, watching him. She'd changed her clothes. He closed his eyes again.

"Time to eat," she said. She was holding him up, spooning soup into his mouth. She'd changed her clothes again. This time she looked worried. He glanced at his useless hands and noticed symbols painted on his palms. He was too weak to ask why they were there. He closed his eyes again.

She was rolling him over. He blinked and rubbed his face. He heard her exhale in relief. "Thank the goddess."

He closed his eyes again.

"Jason? Jason." Selene's short, natural nails shook his shoulder, just below his Fireborn tattoo.

"Haven't you had enough?" he asked, as if she were a lover who wanted another go. He laughed to himself. If only his exhaustion was due to marathon lovemaking.

"What? Jason, you have to wake up."

He rolled over and looked at her, his face falling. "What have you done to me?"

She hesitated. "Do you think you can make it to the bathtub? I've filled it for you, and I'd like you to try to get up. You've been ill."

He tested his limbs, then nodded.

Sitting him up, she swung his legs off the bed and helped him plant his feet. After a few false starts, she looped his arm around her shoulders and helped him to stand. Step by step they made their way to the bathroom where she undressed him like a child and helped him into the tub.

"You had a fever," she said. "A high fever. But it's over now."

"Kill me," he mumbled.

"No. I'm not going to kill you. It's going to be okay."

He shook his head. "You tried to kill me," he said more clearly.

She sighed. "No. I did what I needed to do to start your recovery. I didn't want to hurt you. We were supposed to do that gently, from a relaxed, seated position. In an ideal world, you would have let me in. But you forced my hand when you threatened me."

Jason laid his head back on the side of the tub. "You could have just asked me to stop."

"I did."

He tried to think back, but all he remembered was the wolf, the overwhelming feeling of wanting her. Everything else was a blur, flashes and random images he could barely associate with the woman in front of him. He raised his wet hands to his face.

"I forgive you," Selene said. "Don't waste a second of your recovery thinking about it. I knew what I was getting myself into."

He snorted, rolling his head to the side to give her a pointed glare. "Funny, it seems I didn't."

"As long as you resist treatment, everything we do together is going to feel like a fight, and you're the one who will wear the bruises," she said firmly.

With his eyes tightly closed, Jason asked, "Did you find what you needed? Or did you almost kill me for nothing?"

Selene sat cross-legged on the bathroom floor. "I want to talk about Professor Matthews."

The water splashed as Jason opened his eyes and unsuccessfully tried to sit up. "That's what you decided to dig out of my head? Jill Matthews?"

"She was your trigger. You keep her in the darkest corner of your mind."

He sighed. "Fitting, I guess. If there was one thing Jill had in spades, it was darkness."

"I watched her take advantage of you. It was obvious you didn't want to be there, but she mentioned you... signed up for something."

He leaned his head back again. He remembered, but it wasn't something he liked to talk about. And it had absolutely nothing to do with his vice.

Selene sighed. "She said something that stood out to me. 'We're just two people—'"

"'Taking solace from an unforgiving world in the safety of each other's arms.' I forgot that was something Jill used to say."

"I think it's significant."

"It was a long time ago, long before my vice was a problem."

Selene said nothing, the silence growing weighted between them.

"You won't believe me when I tell you this, but what happened with Matthews started with..." It looked like he was about to make the *J* sound, but he didn't speak her name.

"Jessica?"

He nodded. "She was also a grad student at the same university. I met her at a bar before I realized she was the daughter of the Crescent Star pack alpha. We'd met before, but I didn't remember. Anyway, it turned out she was a TA for one of my classes. Just a weird coincidence." He rubbed his chest. "The beginnings of the mating bond hit us both immediately, but I hadn't claimed her yet. It was too early. We were too young to fully understand what was happening between us. We didn't reject the bond, just hadn't completed it. A few days after we'd met, we were in an office Jessica used for meeting with students when we, uh, got carried away. Professor Matthews walked in on us, Jessica in a compromising position on the desk.

"When Jessica spoke with her, Jill acted like she understood and there would be no repercussions. But then she spoke with me. She said she'd have Jessica fired, unless I agreed."

"You agreed to give her what she wanted in exchange for her silence," Selene whispered.

Jason nodded slowly. "It was a sophisticated trap she'd set for me. At first she wanted only a kiss for her silence. What was one kiss in exchange for Jessica's career? But she'd secretly recorded us. Then she threatened to show Jessica if I didn't take things further. It progressed so fast. Goddess, I hated her."

"So that's what started it."

"No." Jason shook his head. "I was a normal werewolf who enjoyed sex. I didn't suffer from a wolf's vice until…"

"Until that day. I saw you in her office. Silas was trying to call you."

The scene that played out in Jason's head made his stomach turn again, and a wave of exhaustion overcame him. He closed his eyes. "I don't want to talk about this."

"Why was Silas calling you that day?" She lowered herself to her knees next to the tub and folded her arms on the edge, nothing but compassion in her voice.

"Can we take a break? Plenty of time to probe my subconscious and torture me with the results later, right?" He looked at his hands in the water. The symbols she'd drawn there had washed away and turned the bath slightly red.

She didn't waver from her goal. "Why was Silas calling you?"

"I... I'm naked. Can you hand me a towel?"

Selene raised her eyebrows and smiled roguishly. "You weren't wearing one when I put you in there."

"Hide your virgin eyes, woman!" he tried to tease. "Aren't you supposed to maintain your innocence? One look at my member and you'll be ruined for celibacy."

The corner of her mouth twitched up. "Sorry to break it to you, but I had more than an eyeful when I was in your memories, not to mention while I was taking care of you over the past four days. I think I can control myself."

"Four days?" Jason wiped a hand over his face.

She nodded slowly. "By the way, acolytes are celibate —they're not necessarily virgins."

Jason lifted an eyebrow. "Pass the popcorn, someone

has a story to tell. What in the goddess's name are you saying?"

"Tell me why Silas was calling, and I'll get you out of this tub and tell you my story."

He took a deep breath and watched a bead of water roll down the tiled wall. There was no getting around this. She wasn't going to let it drop. "Silas was calling to tell me... my parents had been shot. He called to tell me they were dead and so was Jessica. Alex Bloodright shot her and my parents while I was fucking Jill Matthews."

FIFTEEN

"Which drawer?" Selene drifted to his dresser.

"Third on the left," Jason said. He was sitting naked on the bed, and by the way he swayed, having a hard time remaining upright.

"It's okay if you want to lie down," she said as she retrieved a pair of sweats and a T-shirt.

When she turned back around, he was scowling at her. "Doesn't it bother your acolyte-ness to see me naked?"

"Like I said, most of us had lives before we joined the order. I joined at sixteen. I've seen a dick before."

Jason broke out in a fit of coughing, staring at her as if deeply disturbed by her use of the word *dick*. Well, he could think what he wanted. She had no intention of deceiving him into believing she was somehow better than anyone else. Selene had a past, and if Jason knew that, it might give him the hope that he, too, could overcome his.

She pulled his T-shirt over his head and knelt in front of him to help him into his sweats. Her cheeks grew warm when she found herself eye to eye with the male member they'd just been discussing. Although she hadn't been lying when she'd said she'd seen a dick before, she'd never seen one quite as large or as beautifully made as Jason's. Goddess, nothing about the man was average or unattractive. She stood up, trying her best to hide her body's response to him. He finished pulling them on himself.

"Are you okay?" he asked, with a roguish smile. "You're flushed."

Rolling her eyes, she wiped the back of her hand across her sweating forehead. This would be so much easier if Jason were old or plain or smelled different. Oh goddess, she loved his smell, an earthy concoction of warm cloves and ground chicory that seemed to ooze naturally from his pores. She looked away for a moment.

"I need something to eat, and I know you do too. Can you make it to the kitchen, or do you want me to bring you something in here?"

"I can make it... with your help." He held out a hand to her. She helped him up, and they slowly made their way into the great room, where she propped him in a chair at the dining table. As she moved into the kitchen to start lunch, his silence surprised her. He gave her nothing. No teasing. No insults. No anger.

She'd almost finished frying up some hamburgers when he finally spoke.

"I've spent a long time trying to forget that day," he said.

Selene didn't say anything, just glanced at him and plated the burgers, adding chips along the edge of the plate.

"You must think I'm trash. Royal trash. Nothing but a waste of oxygen."

Her face tightened, and she moved the food to the table. She stared at Jason for a moment, then placed her hands on either side of his face. "Being used by someone does not make you trash. Jill Matthews is trash."

"I should've told Jessica what Matthews was trying to do. I should have brought it all into the light."

"You were trying to save her job, something she loved."

"But to do what I did... I'm a fucking werewolf, the brother of the alpha. I could have snapped her neck, and I let her manipulate me. I'm an idiot. Fucking worthless." Dark circles had appeared under his eyes. He was coming apart.

"No." Selene made him look her in the eye. "You're extraordinary. Because you are going to survive this. You are going to overcome what she did to you. You are not to blame for this evil. She was older. She had the power. And she knew exactly what she was doing. Seemed practiced at it in fact. We all can look back and think of things we should have done, but none of it will change the past. You're going to move beyond this. And I'm going to celebrate every step you take."

For a moment, she was staring straight into his soul,

at a boy who'd hidden so much pain for so long that he didn't know what to do with it now that it was exposed. But like a switch, she watched him change. He camouflaged his despair with a thick blanket of cynicism and that roguish grin that tugged somewhere deep inside her. She slid a hamburger in front of him.

"You owe me a story," he said. "Of how you're not a virgin."

She retrieved two teacups and filled them both with the hot tea she'd made while he was sleeping. Waves of steam twisted from the surface, the scent of lemon and orange blossom filling her nostrils. She didn't want to talk about this with him. She'd promised in the heat of the moment, but now she regretted the offer.

"You should eat something," she said.

To her relief, Jason bit into the burger and seemed to realize just how hungry he was. He finished his first in just a few bites, although he searched her face as if trying to decipher her expression the entire time. "What made you decide to become an acolyte?" he asked as he started in on the next one.

Selene took a long sip of tea and thought about the question. Should she answer it honestly or give him the sanitized version she used in polite conversation? She looked at him over the lip of her teacup. Every time he lifted the burger to his mouth, his hand trembled. He was eating, but he was exhausted. She couldn't deny him the truth, not if she expected him to keep going. She pushed her plate across the table and moved beside him, rather than across from him.

"Can I help you with that?" She reached for the burger.

He shook his head and laughed. "I can feed myself."

"I'll tell you what, if you allow me to help you, I'll tell you the story of how I became an acolyte."

His eyes narrowed, but he seemed to have no fight left in him to argue. With a deep sigh, he gave her one curt nod.

"I wasn't always a member of Fireborn pack." She cut the burger into quarters and raised one to his lips, trying not to think of how intimate the gesture felt.

"I was wondering. I don't remember you as a child or a teen, but then my family..."

"Royalty is often separated from the masses." She lifted the sleeve of her T-shirt to reveal her pack tattoo. "I didn't become a Fireborn until I was sixteen. I believe you were already away at college by then."

"What pack were you with before?" Jason asked, taking another bite from her fingers.

Selene shook her head. "Running solo."

Jason arched an eyebrow. "No pack at all?"

"I was born into a human family. Both my parents were human. The first time I shifted, my father tried to shoot me. I didn't remember, of course. I was fifteen and had a fever. The heat was so extreme I became delirious and stumbled outside into the snow in the middle of the night. I woke up the next morning, naked, shivering, with blood on my face. After I snuck back into the house, my father told my mother that he'd shot at a wolf hanging around our front porch. I didn't know that wolf was me. Not yet."

"You're lucky to be alive. Most werewolves born to human parents don't make it through their first shift."

"I wasn't a genetic anomaly. My mother recognized the signs and told me what I was. The man I thought was my father, wasn't. My mother became pregnant by a werewolf and pawned me off on my human father when the guy hit the road. She didn't even remember his full name."

"Oh, Selene." Jason shook his head.

"The next time I shifted, I did it where both my parents could see. I thought if I brought it out in the open, things would be different. I thought they'd help me. The next day, I left for school. When I came back, they were gone."

"Gone?"

"They moved." Her gaze drifted toward the window. "While I was in class so that they wouldn't have to face me, the only family I'd ever known abandoned me."

"What happened to you? How did you survive?"

"The landlord kicked me out of the house soon after. I lived on the street for a while. Did things I'm not proud of to survive. Stole. Hurt people." She frowned at her plate. "And other things. Whatever I had to do."

Jason's face went slack. He stared at her like he'd never seen her before.

"At first I had this dream that my real father might find me. But eventually I gave up on that idea. I'd shift alone and always shift back alone. And then one day, when I shifted back, a stranger was with me. He insisted I come with him to Rivergate. He introduced me to Artemis, and she took me under her wing. The rest is, as they say, history."

"Who was the man?"

Selene smiled. "Your brother Silas. He'd been out working a case and shifted outside the grounds. His wolf found me."

"Silas?" Jason shifted his narrowed gaze toward the window.

"Afterward, Artemis asked me to join Fireborn since I had no claim to any pack. I accepted and decided soon after that I wanted to be just like Artemis. Besides your brother, she is the only person on this earth I ever fully trusted. The only one I do trust with my life and my soul."

Jason gave her a pitying glance. "You had a rough start."

"It made me value relationships and the role of the goddess in our lives. Finding a home with Fireborn pack made me believe I was destined to follow in Artemis's footsteps."

"You aspire to be the pack priestess."

"All acolytes do."

"Some more than others." He tilted his head.

"There are some who quit early on, but I've been doing this for almost three years now and it's the first time I've felt fully connected to anything. Artemis thinks I may be the one to take over her role when she retires."

Jason selected another piece of burger and brought it

to his mouth on his own. She didn't miss that the tremble was gone. He was already getting stronger now that the food and the tea had had a chance to enter his system.

"You're doing better. I told you that you were hungry," she said.

"Can I ask you something?"

"Something else? I feel like I'm giving you my life history."

"You said I wasn't the first man you'd seen naked."

"You're not."

"When you say you did things to survive…"

Selene sighed. He was going to make her say it. "I had sex in exchange for things, to survive. Sometimes by choice. Sometimes by force. Never a good experience. I don't like to talk about it."

Jason growled.

"It was a long time ago." She lowered her chin and stared at him.

His brows knit, and he shook his head. "I'm sorry, Selene. I almost forced myself on you the other night. I was out of control. It must have been terrifying, especially considering your past." He leaned toward her, his gaze locking with hers. "I'd never hurt you. Not intentionally."

For a long time, she simply stared at him, sizing him up. "I know." She took a bite of her own burger, more certain than ever that her words were true. "Now I've answered your questions. You need to answer mine."

"I thought I did. What other questions could you have?"

Selene nodded. "I feel like I don't have the full story."

Jason glanced toward the balcony. "Come outside with me?"

"Jason..."

"I'll tell you. Just help me outside. If I eat another bite, I'm going to pop. I haven't seen the sun in four days."

She stood and helped him to the balcony, although he barely leaned on her. She had the sense he could have made it on his own. A warm breeze circled her shoulders as she lowered him onto one of the sling-back chairs.

"Do you want me to get you a blanket?" she asked. It was a cold spring day.

"No. I'm okay."

Selene sat down beside him, trying to be patient.

"Considering she was a human, Professor Matthews acted more like a spider. I explained how she drew me in. As you might imagine, I distanced myself from Jessica during this time because I was confused and didn't know what to say to her about what was happening. I'd gotten myself tangled in her web so quickly and thoroughly." He bared his teeth. "But the phone rang three days later and it was her."

"You hadn't spoken to her since it started?" Selene's voice felt thin and weak.

"No. Jessica called to invite me to a charity performance at a theater in Carlton City. She was attending with her parents, the leaders of Crescent Star pack. My parents had already invited me and my siblings to the same event. I said I couldn't go because I couldn't face her after what had happened with Matthews. I told myself I'd use the time to figure out a way to stop it from ever happening again. My sister couldn't go either because she was finishing an intense veterinary medicine program at the time. And Silas couldn't go because he was a new detective and he was working that night." Jason's voice petered out at the end until she could barely hear him. She threaded her fingers into his and squeezed.

"It's understandable. Anyone might do the same in your shoes."

He turned his head to look at her, his green eyes as cutting and bright as emeralds. "The rest is history. My parents, her parents, and Jessica were gunned down in the Harlequin Theater at that performance. That call was the last time I heard Jessica's voice. Not only did I miss Silas's call to tell me they were dead, but I possibly missed my last chance to have a true mate, a fated mate. I never spoke to my parents after that day either. The memory you saw, that was the day my wolf broke. I felt it happen like a snap. My inner beast is feral, Selene. It's why I didn't want you here, no matter how much I believed you could help. You can't trust me, ever. Inside, I'm broken." He lifted a hand to his chest. "My wolf is damaged. Irreparable."

Selene's lips parted, and she took a tiny sip of air, trying her best not to react to the revelation, not to feel the aching pain that rolled off Jason like a fog and settled right over her heart. The look on his face said it all. He loathed himself. Loathed what he'd done.

Standing from her chair, Selene knelt in front of him on the concrete, placing her hands on top of his.

"You couldn't have known what would happen. It isn't your fault."

"No? Maybe if I'd had a spine. If I'd stood up to her… maybe I would have gone with Jessica to that stupid play, and maybe I could have stopped Alex."

"Maybe. Or you might have been another of his victims. Jessica was a potential mate. That means she wanted the best for you, just like you did for her. If she were here, I believe that she, like your parents, would feel happy you survived. If they were here, they'd tell you they forgive you for that day and many others. They'd want you to forgive yourself."

"How do you know?" Jason's green eyes were wet with unshed tears.

"I'm an acolyte, Jason." Selene squeezed his hands. "Goddess willing, it's my job to know."

CHAPTER
SIXTEEN

Jason's head pounded like the drum line in a subpar marching band. He'd hoped he could work a little, knew that after four days his inbox would be full, but after staring at a single email for the better part of an hour, he conceded he wasn't ready.

Shuffling from his room, he found Selene curled in the leather chair with one of the books from the library in the guest room. She didn't appear to be reading it, however. Her violet eyes stared past the page seemingly lost in a daydream.

"How about a movie?" Jason asked.

"Please." She closed the book. "If you're not too tired. It's getting late."

"I've spent days in bed." He grimaced. "I have no desire to go back there. Not yet."

"What do you want to watch?"

"I have every streaming service known to man. Pick your poison."

She snagged the remote off the coffee table and turned on the television. He watched her fold her legs underneath her on the sofa as she flipped through her options. What would she pick? Did acolytes even watch TV?

"Here we go." She clicked on an icon and tossed the remote back on the coffee table.

Jason smiled. "*The Lord of the Rings*? A strange choice for an acolyte."

"It's a classic! What do you think acolytes should watch?"

"*The Sound of Music*," Jason responded immediately.

Selene's mouth dropped open. "You do understand I don't make my own clothes from my curtains."

He raised a brow at her thrift-store jeans and T-shirt combo. "You paid for that?"

She gasped in feigned outrage. "Not everyone needs or can afford monogrammed dress shirts, *Prince* Jason. How much did you pay for the privilege of looking like a pretentious asshat?" She flipped him the bird.

Laughing, he crossed the room to sit at the other end of the sofa. "I just think you're beautiful and deserve beautiful clothes. Maybe I need to make a donation to Sanctuary. Artemis needs to take better care of her acolytes."

Her body tensed. Perhaps she was remembering the way he'd thrown her against the wall. Jason was probably like a dark cave to her. Once you'd seen the bear go in, even if you never saw it again, you'd never trust the darkness. You'd assume the bear was in there, hiding in the shadows.

She scooted away from him, closer to the armrest. "How are you feeling?"

Jason leaned his head back and analyzed her body language. Yep, she was afraid. Goddess, he owed her one. "My wolf is still making demands, but he's not as loud inside my head as he used to be. Actually, when I think about what I did to you, it makes me feel ill. It was uncalled for. It won't happen again."

Selene glanced at her fingers tangled in her lap. "Then we accomplished our goal. You've seen your vice for what it is."

"So that's it? I'm cured?"

She snorted. "No. Not yet. Your vice will grow stronger with time, but the more you practice pushing it away, the longer it will stay away."

"What's the next step of the program?" he asked.

"I'll teach you coping techniques—meditation, anchoring—so when it does happen, you'll be ready. You can do this, Jason. The hardest part is over."

"Thank you." His eyes met hers. All he could think was that she was the most beautiful woman he'd ever known. Not sexy, but beautiful, down to her very soul.

"You're welcome."

Jason leaned back against the sofa, and for the first time in forever, he felt truly *with* a woman. As he glanced over at her, taking her in while she watched the movie, his chest swelled with respect and admiration. When this was all over, he hoped they'd stay friends, even after she became a priestess.

"Jason?" She turned and his heart leaped when her gaze fell on him.

"Yes?"

"This is the most uncomfortable couch I've ever sat on." She shifted awkwardly.

"Admittedly." He chuckled.

"It feels like I'm sitting on a burlap bag full of ball bearings."

"Completely uncomfortable." He nodded.

She spread her hands in confusion. "Why do you own this?"

He shrugged. "Someone told me it was the best."

"Someone lied to you." She started laughing. "Never trust that person again."

He was laughing with her when his phone rang. "I've got to take this." He rose and scrambled from the couch, jogging out onto the balcony for some privacy. As he watched Selene through the glass door, he answered the call.

"Hey, stranger. What are you doing tonight? I haven't seen you at the club in weeks."

"Samantha?" Jason asked. He'd had an on-again, off-again affair with the redhead for years. "No, I can't make it out tonight."

There was silence on the other end of the line. "Are you feeling okay?"

"Yeah, I'm fine. You could say I'm just tired of the club scene."

"Do you want me to come to your place?"

"No," Jason said quickly.

She scoffed. "What's going on? Don't take this the wrong way, but this is the first time I've ever called you that you weren't interested in meeting up. Please tell me you don't have cancer or some awful disease."

Somewhere above him, a bird flapped its wings as it landed on the roof. Jason stared at it, admiring the flight, the freedom. "I've just decided... I need more."

The call went quiet except for the sound of her breath.

"Samantha?"

"Good luck finding whatever you're after." The call ended.

Jason watched Selene through the glass, smiling as she slid from the uncomfortable couch to sit on the floor. For the hundredth time that day, he wished that things could be different, that she wasn't an acolyte and that he didn't have a vice.

His phone call was over, but he didn't rush to go back in. Instead, he rested his head against the window and just watched her.

Selene was curious about what was taking Jason so long on the phone. She supposed it was work related. He had been unconscious for most of four days. When he finally did return, he didn't bother with the sofa but sat down beside her on the floor. His hand landed on the carpet mere centimeters from hers, the outside of her pinky warming from the heat coming off his golden flesh. Her pulse should not have quickened, and her attention should not have lingered on the way his dark hair curved along his temple, accentuating the hard angles of his face.

No, she should have been afraid, afraid his wolf could smell the arousal she was suppressing. Afraid he'd break his resolve and push her against the couch the same way he'd pushed her against the wall. But that wasn't what she was afraid of. Her true fear, the one that lingered deep within, the one she'd toppled the bookcases and furniture of her mind to stop from reaching her, was that she wanted him to do it again. The memory of his body on hers and the thought that he *could* want only her were ideas so erotic they held a seductive power strong enough to make her temporarily forget her goal to become priestess.

His nostrils flared, but he didn't look at her. He watched, unblinking, as Frodo pressed his hobbit-back into the dirty nook under the road and closed his eyes against the temptation to put on the ring even as the Ringwraith hovered over his head.

Selene pulled her hand into her lap.

SEVENTEEN

"Stop fidgeting," Selene said, glancing at Jason. The east-facing balcony was bathed in the warming light of sunrise, but the calming effect of the blue skies and singing birds above seemed lost on him. His face gleamed with fresh sweat, and he squirmed on the yoga mat as if he were sitting on a bed of nails.

A few days had passed since she'd found his trigger. He was stronger now. He could handle more. But the wolf was back this morning with a vengeance.

They'd been experimenting with intense exercise to work off the extra physical energy related to his vice, making use of his home gym several hours a day. But all the push-ups and miles on the treadmill hadn't seemed to placate Jason's wolf today. Clearly he wanted sex. His entire body seemed to protest for it. Selene needed to find another way to help him.

"How is this supposed to work again?" he asked.

"Take a deep breath, close your eyes, and begin the

mantra I taught you. Let it pull you down into deep meditation. It will help with your withdrawal symptoms."

His shoulders slumped, his presence heavy beside her. "Every time I close my eyes, I see…"

"You see what?"

"I see myself attacking you, grabbing you by the throat, pushing you against the wall."

Selene glanced toward the door. "Now? You're fantasizing about this now?"

"No! I'm not fantasizing, I'm remembering. That night, when I forced you to let me go to the bordello… I realize now, you don't want to be here any more than I do. You certainly don't want my disgusting hands all over your body. *Fuck.*" He scrubbed his face, turning slightly away from her. "I couldn't help myself, Selene, and how I felt then, I feel that now. You should leave before my wolf makes me do something we'd both regret."

There was a long stretch of silence. "Jason… Jason, look at me." She reached over and tugged his chin so that he faced her, although his gaze remained focused on a segment of the balcony railing over her right shoulder. "When I took this assignment, I expected that your vice would take control at some point. I was prepared. You're dealing with intense withdrawal. It's to be expected."

"No." He shook his head. "I'm dangerous. You don't understand, I liked the feel of you against me. My skin is crawling for want of it." He pushed off the mat and paced to the other side of the balcony. "What if it happens again and I can't stop? After what you've been through in your past..." He shook his head.

"My past is in my past. You are not responsible for what happened to me." It was true that part of her still feared Jason on some level, and on an even deeper level, another part of her had enjoyed his touch. Saying either of those things out loud, however, wouldn't help him get better or earn her a promotion to *Preotka*. She had to stay objective. "You know firsthand that I can defend myself. I knocked you on your ass for four days."

"Yes."

"Literally knocked you into tomorrow."

"Yes."

"I can do it again."

"Please don't."

"The important thing is you didn't try to slit my throat when you woke up. You were barely angry with me."

"What good would it do to be angry at you for defending yourself from..." He pointed his hands at himself.

"That means on some level you want to get better. You understand what we're doing here and want to succeed."

"Or I just feel disgusting for throwing myself at you."

She moistened her lips. "You're not disgusting," she said. "You have a problem and we're fixing it. That's all. You won't hurt me."

A storm moved in behind Jason's eyes, his irises morphing from green to amber, the color of his wolf's.

He clung to the railing behind him with a white-knuckled death grip as if it were the only thing keeping him from attacking her. The darkness was back. He was a predator again.

"You don't know what you do to me. Even now, I want to press myself against you. I want to feel the heat of your skin on my tongue. I want to run my hand up the inside of your thigh." He looked her straight in the eye, and he seemed taller than a moment before. The intensity of his stare made her shiver. "Don't tell me it's okay. Tell me you understand the risks of being here and that you forgive me for wanting you."

Chest tight, Selene held his gaze. She hoped the mild breeze masked her arousal as the images he painted in her brain quickened her breath. "I... I forgive you," she said. "And I know it could happen again... but I don't think it will. You can control yourself. What I'm teaching you today will help."

For a long time, he simply stared at her, breathing in and out. In and out. Slowly his amber eyes turned green again. He lowered himself to the mat, crossed his legs, and straightened his spine.

"Close your eyes," she said quietly. He did. With a deep, cleansing breath, Selene centered herself. "Let's try again."

This time Jason got it right. The space beside her grew quiet and cool. His fidgeting stopped. Her ears lost the thump of his racing heart. But he'd need help to go deeper, to that place of healing she knew he must go. That's where she came in.

Closing her eyes, she threaded her fingers into his, ignoring the way the touch of his hand sent a warm current of heat up her arm. He must have felt it too because his body stiffened. She began her mantra.

Meditation was a grounding force in Selene's life, a way of centering herself that had saved her from the shame of being homeless and the shame of all the things she'd done to survive. It had helped her transition into the order and strengthened her mind. Desperately, she wanted to give Jason this tool to ease the suffering she'd seen in him. She reached out from her center, psychically surrounded him, and lowered him into that space between sleep and awake.

In that wide-open consciousness, color, emotion, and pure mindfulness were all that existed. The muddy-green color of his aura became palpable, clouding the pale blue of her own. Jason's aura was dark, but at the heart of it, a spark of bright green burned, crystal clear and lit from within. This was what she was trying to save. This was Jason. The real Jason.

She gripped his hand tighter, her bright blue light coming to rest next to his bright green one. And that's where she stayed. There was nothing sexual about the encounter, but there could be nothing more intimate. Her soul rested with his in a place beyond time or space. They revolved around each other, two stars orbiting, held in the other's gravitational pull.

When it was time to kick off the bottom and float back to the real world, Selene had to do the kicking. She'd practiced this. It would take Jason time to learn to go this deep and know when it was time to come back to reality.

She smiled as she broke the surface. But when she turned to check on Jason, her breath hitched in her throat. His face was serene, all the fear, longing, and bitterness his body had held only moments ago replaced by a deep peace. He'd even stopped sweating.

She opened her hand, releasing his fingers. No tremors. No pain. No wanting. The muscles of his jaw were relaxed. She almost hated to bring him out of it, but the beneficial effects would diminish if he stayed where he was. Softly she whispered his name, "Jason."

HE WAS SAFE. SAFE AND WARM AND CARED FOR. THERE WAS NO endless wanting, no bottomless pit of shame or ache of need. And the source of this serenity was in his hand, nestled between his fingers. Then it was gone.

Desperate to return to that place of peace, he tried to reach for the hand again. But she denied him. He opened his eyes. There was an angel hovering over him, a bright blue angel with the sunrise spilling through a curtain of her hair like liquid gold. For a moment, he lost himself in the connection they shared. Pure light poured into his heart and filled him. He wasn't alone.

"Welcome back," the angel said. Selene. Her name was Selene.

And then the blue faded and his hands began to shake again. His tongue stuck to the roof of his parched mouth. A muscle in his leg cramped to the point of pain, and a hardcore throb began between his temples as if a little man were building a railroad between his eyes.

"I need a drink."

"How about an aspirin?" She held out her hand to help him up.

The corner of his mouth lifted, and he shook his head. "I think I'd better get up on my own." He avoided her touch as he stood.

She sighed and let him go.

WEEKS LATER, JASON WOKE, KNOWING THE FULL MOON WAS just around the corner. It was a good thing he'd made slow and steady progress with Selene's help, because his wolf would be close to the surface today. In two days, he'd have to endure the shift and face dozens of women he'd slept with at Rivergate. He'd thrown himself into his therapy with the same determination and fortitude he'd always devoted to his business. And he was healing. Controlling himself around Selene was getting easier, despite wanting her every minute of the day. They'd fallen into a kind of routine, a routine he could get used to.

This morning, as usual, he drifted to the coffee machine while Selene started chopping vegetables for omelets. He'd just filled the water reservoir when she said something that chilled him to the bone. "I think we should try aura manipulation again today."

Aura manipulation. That's what she'd done to him before, the thing that had almost killed him. His neck craned and his eyes locked onto hers. "Why? I thought you found the source of my vice the first time. If there's something more, I sure as hell don't know what it is."

"My first time in your psyche, I was looking for the source of the darkness within you. This time I want to look for the source of the light, an anchor you can hold on to if you feel like you might lose control. If you become aware of what strengthens your soul and you foster it, Nickelova's curse won't be able to take root in you. If she comes back, she won't be able to control you."

He switched on the coffeepot, then realized he'd forgotten to add coffee and switched it back off. As he pulled the ground beans from the pantry, he asked, "What if you can't find any light in me? What if you drift down my light bulb aisle and find nothing but an assortment of coal and cinders?"

She snorted. "You have light. I saw it while we were meditating. I just couldn't see the source. It's bright green. Your soul is beautiful."

Jason stared at her for a moment. "Is yours blue?"

She nodded excitedly. "Yes! Yes. You saw it? That's really good, Jason. The scrolls say that if you can sense someone's aura, you're in the presence of the goddess herself. That type of meditation is as good as a prayer."

"The goddess, huh?" He took a deep breath. "I never actually believed in the goddess. I'm still not sure there isn't another explanation for what you do."

"How do you explain how I saved you from the curse?

I'm not a witch. My only power comes from my connection to the goddess through our religious order."

His brow furrowed. "How *did* you lift my curse?"

"I didn't lift it exactly. I performed a ritual asking the goddess to transfer it into me." She pointed at her chest.

"Then why aren't you catatonic in bed like I was?"

"My training and lifestyle keep me pure. Nickelova's curse was attached to your vice, but when I transferred it into me, there was no place for it to take root. It fizzled and died like a seed on concrete."

"Your innocence saved you."

"I told you last night, I'm not exactly innocent, but my way of life is powerful."

"Hmmm." It had been a long time since he'd thought of the goddess or his place in the universe. What was it about Selene? Every moment he spent with her challenged him to be a better person. "Thank you for risking yourself for me."

Selene blushed and turned toward the frying pan.

"Are you all right? Did I say something wrong?"

She plated the eggs. "Just fine. Let's eat. I want to get started as soon as possible."

EIGHTEEN

To say that Jason was apprehensive about Selene entering his memories again was an understatement. The first time had felt like having his heart pulled out of his nostril, chewed up, and spit back into the opposite nostril. Silas had been right. The woman sitting cross-legged before him looked as sweet and gentle as an angel, but the power in those dainty, tapered fingers, those two hands adorned with ritualistic symbols, was as fierce and powerful as the goddess's.

"You're trembling again," Selene said. "Are the withdrawal symptoms coming back?"

"No."

"Then what's wrong?"

"I'm scared shitless. I don't want to end up in bed for four days again."

She took one of his hands in hers, and Jason had to suppress the temptation to pull her forward the extra inch and press his lips to hers. "Trust me, Jason. Last time I was rough with you. I had to be. You were fighting me at every turn. This time it won't be like that. You know why we're doing this now. You've already come so far. Open yourself up to me."

He nodded. What other choice did he have? Her hand on his might as well have been a steel binding. His heart would have skipped out of his chest and slid down his arm to be part of that coupling, the traitor.

"The only way to conquer a vice is to discover the need it's trying to fill and fill it with something else. Today I'm going to find a memory of something that once filled that need, before your vice took hold. One so bright and powerful it will become an anchor, holding you to your true need, keeping you from floating too far toward your vice."

"Okay. Why can't I remember it on my own?"

"Believe it or not, our minds have a way of shielding us from the good as well as the bad. I'll be able to remind you of things you may not recall on your own." Adjusting herself so that her knees touched his, she moved her hands to hover over his heart. "Ready?"

"Yes," he said. He wasn't ready. Not really. But he trusted her.

She closed her eyes and gently touched his chest.

THE MOMENT HER HANDS TOUCHED JASON, SELENE FELT THE familiar spinning as if the rate of the earth revolving on its axis increased threefold. The great room melted away, and she stood in the infinite web of pulsing strands that made up his memories. With a jolt, she noticed the dark tangle she'd visited before—the memory of Professor Matthews—was lighter in color now, the strands still coiled tightly but not tied in knots like before. He'd accepted the events and was starting to heal emotionally. Good.

She scanned the web, looking for the light. Bright green pulsed above her, and she followed it toward a particularly bright spot in his consciousness.

But when she found the brightest, warmest spot in his memories, she had trouble reaching it. It was all tangled up and hidden by dark sections so that she almost couldn't tell where the light began and the darkness ended. Reaching out, she folded her hand to navigate the knot until, with surgical precision, her fingers slid over the argent thread at its center. Blinding light surrounded her, transported her, and she found herself standing in a kitchen.

Baking gingerbread filled the air with the scent of molasses and warm spices, and the laughter of three teenage siblings met her ears. She knew these kids. The royal family: Silas, Jason, and Laina. Which meant that the woman swaying and humming in front of the stove was their mother. A white candle inside a glass hurricane lamp burned brightly between them, surrounded by an arrangement of greens, red berries, and ribbon. *Christmas,* she thought.

"You should take French, Jason. The girls love a man who can speak French," Silas said. He looked to be eighteen or nineteen and was wearing a Cornell T-shirt.

"Silas," the dark-haired girl said, rolling her eyes. That was Laina, his sister. "Jason shouldn't choose a language to study based on its ability to woo girls. He should be thinking about college and employment opportunities." Laina rubbed the youngest boy's shoulders. "Study Spanish or, better yet, Mandarin."

Their mother left the stove to plant a kiss on the side of Jason's head. "Choose what speaks to your heart. If you follow your passion, the universe will find the right place for you." She ruffled his hair before crossing back to the stove to pull the tray of cookies from the oven.

"Mom, that's terrible advice!" Laina said. "Who knows what stupid ideas his heart will come up with? He could end up wasting his time on something utterly useless, like... like Italian."

A lanky man with glasses and a hint of gray in his hair strode in and spun Mrs. Flynn around. *"Cosa c'è di sbagliato con l'italiano?"*

Mrs. Flynn looked up into her husband's eyes and adjusted her arms around his neck. She took a deep, contented breath. "Personally, I love Italian," she whispered into her husband's lips. The two parents danced between the oven and the kitchen island, drawn into each other as if they were the only two people on the planet.

Silas groaned. "Ugh! Get a room." He cupped a hand over his eyes and exchanged awkward glances with his siblings.

"I have a room," Mr. Flynn said through a barely restrained smile. "I have an entire house. You just happen to live in it." They broke into laughter as he spun Mrs. Flynn from his arms.

After a short peck on her husband's cheek, she grabbed the tray of cookies and slid them onto the island. "Who's ready for gingerbread?"

The three teens popped up, and Jason pried a cookie from the tray, tossing it between his hands to keep his fingers from burning. His face... Selene couldn't look away. He was so open, so innocent, so trusting. But the predominant feeling, as she stood in this memory, was love. Unconditional love. Familial love.

This was it. This was his anchor.

As the memory ended, Selene experienced the familiar rushing fall of her extraction from his consciousness with mixed emotions. She desperately wanted to stay in that kitchen, in that safe place of love and warmth, but it wasn't her life or her memory. It was Jason's. Her job was to share it with him, to remind him of the place of love that he came from, the thing he could cling to when the darkness was close at hand.

Opening her lungs, she took a gasping breath as she broke the surface of deep consciousness. Only after removing her hands from Jason's chest did she remember she was the only thing holding him up. He slumped toward her.

"Shoot. Sorry." Catching him by the shoulders, she lowered him to the floor, noticing the thick cords of muscle in his arms. He'd gained weight during their time together. He was bigger. Heavier. "Jason?"

He blinked up at her as if waking from a deep sleep. "Did you get it? Do I have... light?"

"Yes." She laughed. "You have a strong anchor, a memory so perfect I didn't want to leave it."

He pushed himself up on his elbows.

"You should have something to eat and drink. Was it as bad as last time? Do you feel nauseated?"

Jason sat up the rest of the way and rubbed the back of his neck. "Not as bad. I'm groggy, but I feel okay."

"Come on, I'll make you some tea." She held out her hand to him, but he rose without her help. He moved past her to the kitchen where he began filling the teapot.

"So what was this memory?" he asked. He placed the teapot on the stove and lit the burner.

"You were fifteen, in the kitchen with Laina and Silas. Your mother was making gingerbread cookies." Selene paused because Jason had gone ghost white. "What's wrong?"

"Nothing. I... I think... excuse me." He strode from the room without another word, leaving Selene staring confusedly into an empty kitchen.

NINETEEN

Jason flopped on his bed. Why had it been that memory? As soon as Selene had mentioned the cookies, the day had come back to him, a day he'd felt truly loved. It was one of the last days they were all together. Weeks later, Silas would move back to college, and although there would be visits, they would never live under the same roof again.

His stomach flipped as he remembered his parents dancing in the kitchen. It was something they'd done often, a quirky thing he'd found embarrassing as a teenager and oddly out of character for his usually stoic father. Now he'd do anything to see his parents dancing.

Outside his room, he heard Selene digging through his cupboards, pots and pans banging together, cabinet doors opening and closing. He should get up and help her find whatever she was looking for, but he didn't. He was too busy trying to forget the memory she'd recalled in him. What she didn't understand was that his happiest memory was now his most brutal reminder of his parents' murder.

How could he tell Selene that remembering the source of the light within him was what fueled the darkness? A spray of bullets stole that moment from him in the most brutal way possible, negating it and every happy moment that came before. It was a memory of how everything you loved turned to shit eventually. Worm fodder.

And there was something else. The entire time he was thinking about the cookies and the horrible night that ended it all, he didn't think of Jessica once. Not until now. Pieces had come together for him. She'd been his potential mate, but he'd never loved her. He hadn't had a chance to. And although he'd sanctified that relationship and blamed her death for his vice, he realized now that it was more complex than that. Alex had stolen far more than people he'd loved; he'd stolen his childhood, because Jason couldn't feel the joy of those memories without the pain of their loss. And his wolf, with his simplistic feral language of instincts and hungers, had known only one way to numb the pain of it all.

He breathed through a tightness in his throat as he contemplated it, wanting nothing more than to push it all down into the dark abyss of his mind again. Suddenly exhausted, he threaded his fingers behind his head, closed his eyes, and forced himself to forget again as he drifted away.

GINGERBREAD. THE SCENT WAS UNMISTAKABLE AND ALMOST overwhelming to his hypersensitive wolf senses. Immediately the memory came back to him, all its light and its resulting darkness filling him at once.

"Selene, what have you done?" He scowled. Bounding from the bed, he burst from his room, ready to give her a piece of his mind. But when he reached the kitchen, the sight of her thawed any ice that had formed around his heart.

She'd donned a dress, the first one he'd ever seen her wear, simple and conservative with a flowing skirt that reached below the knee. Her hair was down, loose curls draped over her shoulders and flowing to the center of her back. And her smile was bright enough to light up the room.

All he could think was that she was perfect, beautiful, and worthy like an angel dropped down from heaven. Selene pulled a tray of cookies from the oven and turned her violet eyes on him.

"Who's ready for some cookies?" she said softly.

Jason's throat constricted and a muscle in his jaw twitched. Eyes burning, he crossed to her, a confusing mix of emotions swirling in his head. He shook her by the shoulders.

"Oww. Jason, you're hurting me."

A growl emanated from his chest, his wolf lowering its head and baring its teeth. Her eyes widened. This close with his hands wrapped around her upper arms, he was more than aware how his size dwarfed hers. He'd gained the weight back, thanks to her, and now he was using it against her.

Justifiably.

She had yanked his chain one too many times.

"Why would you do this?" he said. "Why would you do this to me?"

"I... I thought you needed help remembering. I wanted to re-create the moment. Sometimes a smell can bring it back." She squirmed within his too-tight grip.

"I remember, Selene. I remember everything about that day," he said through his teeth. "But did it ever occur to you that that memory holds nothing but pain for me?"

Tears formed in her eyes. "You're hurting me," she whispered.

He shook her harder. "They're dead. Every time I think of how perfect our family was, I remember what Alex took from me. He's still out there somewhere, probably being nursed back to health by an evil dragon bitch, and everything that was right and good about my life is gone. Think about what this means. You are telling me that my core memory, the thing that brings light to my soul, is something I can never have again. How can you believe for a second that I can ever leave my vice behind when the darkness is the only thing holding me together? There's no hope for anything else. Everything that was good about me is dead."

Trembling, Selene twisted from Jason's grip. A tear

slipped from the corner of her eye, carving a path down the slope of her nose to her upper lip. "Everything good about you is *not* dead," she said softly. "I wouldn't be here if I thought the light in you had died." She rubbed her shoulders, backing away. "Alex didn't take everything from you. There are still people who believe in you. People who need you."

"Like who?"

"Silas... and Laina."

Jason rolled his eyes.

"The pack. All the people whose businesses you invest in."

"Silas is more alpha than any pack needs, including ours. And you don't need light in your soul to make a good investment."

"Me." Selene's gaze lifted to his. "I need you." Her voice was as brittle as a dried bone.

He licked his lips. "Yeah. You need me to get better so you can be promoted to priestess." He snorted derisively.

"No. That's not it." Selene's voice was laden with emotion as if she were on the verge of tears.

"Then why?"

"Because... because..." She shook her head.

He began to turn, to walk away. Her hand landed on his. Selene guided one hand around her waist and his other into her upturned grip. Jason didn't fight her as she pulled him into her chest.

"Selene, what are you doing?"

Without answering, she began to sway. It took a moment for him to take the lead, for her movement to stop battling his stillness, but soon their bodies moved as one. He rocked back and forth, turning her as they crossed the floor, and never breaking eye contact. He tried not to think about the fact she was an acolyte and his spiritual advisor or that everything that was happening fell well within the bounds of "inappropriate." He was greedy, and the tiny slice of happiness Selene was offering was not something he was willing to turn away.

He held her closer, his face a breath away from hers, and then, without warning, spun her away from his chest, across the kitchen, and back into his arms, dipping her in front of the stove. She giggled, her laugh ringing through him like a bell and lifting two tons of weight from his heart.

"You're stunning," he whispered in her ear as if it were a secret. "Do you know you could have any man you ever wanted with a wink of your eye?"

"Don't be silly," she said breathlessly. "I've never been beautiful."

"Oh, Selene, you're wrong about that, and if you were mine, I'd never let you forget it."

She met his eyes, her lip tucking between her teeth in a gesture that made her look younger than she was. He stood her on her own two feet, realizing his wolf's interest in her had grown to unsafe levels for both of them. As much as he wanted her, as much as he longed to have her goodness in his life permanently, he needed to accept that she was here in a professional capacity only. She might remain friendly with him when all was said and done, but she'd never be his. Not really.

But then why wasn't she moving away from his open arms?

A CHILL CAME OVER SELENE'S BODY AS JASON SET HER ON HER feet and opened his arms, the absence of his touch like the loss of heat after the setting sun. His green eyes darkened, a storm gathering in his thoughts, the irises tinged with amber. In that moment, she was not an acolyte or a spiritual therapist. She was just a woman whose entire being wanted to be back in those arms, wanted to feel *precious* again, wanted a taste of something she'd never had before, never would have again.

She stepped into his space and rose up on her tiptoes, her arms snaking around his neck. His breath quickened with his pulse, his hands spreading wider as if he were afraid to touch her, and his face, oh goddess, his face was a mask of torment. Ignoring the alarms going off in her head, she planted a kiss on his lips. She'd never kissed a man like this. Sure she'd had a mouth forced upon hers. She'd been kissed. But she'd never done the kissing. And certainly a kiss had never felt like this one. Soft, warm, gentle, searching. Her mind blanked, wrapped up in all the emotions and raw feelings that came with her wanton exploration.

But the kiss was one-sided, his body stiff, his lips accepting but tentative. Until, quite suddenly, the wall she'd been pressing against, the invisible thing holding him back, shattered. His arms wrapped around her ribs and swept her away, the storm she'd seen gathering in his eyes swirling around her. The full force of his masculinity beat against her lips, blew across her skin, and doused her body in a deluge of heat. His hands were in her hair, on her waist.

And he was inside her mouth, stroking her tongue with his own in a way that set her on fire. His body pressed against hers, ushering her toward the sofa. When she bumped into its rounded back, he lifted her, hoisting her dress so he could slide between her knees.

Was this really happening? His body held a coiled tension she instinctively knew she could release. If she didn't know better, she'd say it was magic, this force driving them toward each other. She wrapped her arms tighter around his neck, drawing him closer until she could feel the hard length of him pressed against her.

Jason pulled back, panting and groaning as if he were in pain. "No. No, we can't."

Selene shook her head. "This is right. It's all right." Something in the back of her mind knew she was wrong, but she didn't want to think about it. Not now. Not yet. She wanted to stay in the storm, feel the rain drench her face, get swept away by the wind and the lightning without a thought to the consequences.

"You'd regret it. It would mean the end of your acolyte status. And as much as I want you, and oh, by the goddess, I want you, I can't do that to you. I can't take your virtue when I know you'd never do this if I hadn't been such a shit to you and drawn you into my web."

"Drew me in? I wasn't drawn in. I have feelings for you—"

"You're sweet and naive. You don't see it. I'm a predator. I have a power over women. It's not your fault. Without even realizing it, I seduced you. You'd never do this if I hadn't. You'd never risk your future." He backed away, his hands coming to rest on his knees, the physical hardship of holding back the desires of his wolf evident on his face.

Selene's eyes widened, and she looked out the glass doors to the balcony, to the moon that hung in the night sky. "I'm so sorry, Jason. I'm a fool."

"It's not you."

"No. The shift is tomorrow night. I've tempted you at your most vulnerable."

He took a step back, still hunched over, and clutched his middle.

"Are you in pain?"

"Go into your room and lock the door," he said.

"What? Jason, no. Let's talk about this."

He raised his eyes to hers, and all she saw was the animal, the intense need turning his eyes from green to the amber of his wolf's. She hopped down from the back of the couch.

"Go," he said, a deep growl emanating from his chest.

She did, running into her room and locking the door. She heard him pacing on the other side for some time, the slam of what she assumed was the cookie sheet against the counter, the whine of the front door opening, and his groans as Silas's command kept him from leaving.

Eventually, after what seemed like hours of painful pacing, his bedroom door slammed and she heard his shower turn on.

Selene fell back onto her bed, wondering at the ache in her body that accompanied her thoughts of Jason. She ran her fingers down her neck, between her breasts, over the cotton bodice of her dress, and up along her inner thigh. She stopped at the lace edge of her briefs. Was a vice catching? Because right now all Selene could think of, although she knew it was wrong and self-destructive, was how she didn't regret kissing Jason.

If anything, she regretted stopping.

TWENTY

"You finished the cookies," Selene said, setting down the brown plaid suitcase she'd been holding. Sun streamed in through the east-facing windows, but it did nothing to warm her.

Jason gave her an exhausted smile before his eyes locked on her bag. "What's with the suitcase?"

"I think you proved last night that you don't need me anymore. You have full control over your vice. Tonight is the shift. If you can deny yourself so close to the full moon, there's nothing left for me to teach you."

"Oh, I'm not sure about that," he murmured.

She shook her head and looked at the floor.

"For one, I need someone to show me how to make the cookies you made last night. I've never baked anything like that. And someone to hold my hand when I feel sick like you did. Someone to remind me of happy memories. Someone to fill this place with joy and light like you have." He stood and approached her.

"I suspect you'll have no trouble finding a woman to do all those things. And when the time is right and Nickelova is dead, you can build a life with her."

"But she won't be you."

"She can't be me." Selene swallowed the lump that had formed in her throat. "No matter how badly I want that."

Jason took another step toward her, his hands spread as if approaching a skittish animal. "You want this too?" He searched her face. "You feel it too. The bond?" He rubbed his chest.

She had felt it. "I do." Averting her gaze, she chose to be honest. "It feels like there's an energy between us, a magnetism."

"Then why are you leaving?"

"You don't want *me*, Jason. It's natural for a man like you to attach to a caregiver. But once you're back out in the world, you'll realize I'm nothing special. I'm no one, just an orphan living among your pack. And my feelings for you, there's no way to separate them from what happened here."

"You're wrong—"

"My work here is done. If I stay now, I'd only be fostering a dependence we'd both have to break."

He shook his head. "No. That's not what this is. You know that's not what this is."

"I give you permission to leave. You're free. You've graduated from my care. I'll let Silas know, and I'll see you at Rivergate for the shift tonight." She lifted her bag and headed for the door.

"Selene?"

She paused, turning back to him.

"Thank you. I'd be dead if it wasn't for you. I'll never forget that."

With a soft smile and a nod, she said, "In some ways, I could say the same." She slipped out the door and left Jason standing in his foyer.

SELENE RETURNED TO SANCTUARY feeling numb. SHE WAS doing the right thing. Of course she was. The feelings she'd felt for Jason were a natural extension of the therapy she'd administered. Therapists of all kinds were at risk of falling in love with their patients. She'd seen his darkest parts and his happiest memories. She'd shared things about herself she'd never shared with anyone. In time, she'd get on with her real life and those memories would shed like an old snakeskin to some recess of her mind.

When that happened, when she started to forget how happy she was with Jason, how even when he was sick or angry or nearly dead his smile had lit up her soul. When those memories dulled, the pain in her chest would stop and she'd be thankful she was strong today. A person needed to be logical about these things. Love and sex and loneliness were tricky, all mashed up with one another. Time and distance would sort it out.

She rocked backward to fling her suitcase onto the bed, her long skirt catching on the corner. She smoothed the material down, then unzipped her bag to start unpacking. She'd had the plaid brown monstrosity since she was a kid. It had served her well. But maybe this time it would stay unpacked.

"Welcome back," Artemis said from behind her. "I thought I saw you coming through the gate."

Selene smiled. "It's good to be home again." She accepted Artemis's embrace.

"I assume your return is a positive sign. Was your mission effective?"

"Jason has complete control over his vice. I am confident he has been successfully rehabilitated."

"Hmm." Artemis nodded. "I knew you were the right choice for this assignment. Congratulations. A novice acolyte could not have performed the deep spiritual cleansing you did."

Eyes focused on the folded clothes within her suitcase, Selene hummed affirmatively.

"Why do I sense unhappiness within you?"

"Artemis, I have to tell you something. I... made a mistake last night. Or maybe you might call it an accident. There was an accident."

The older woman steadied Selene's trembling hands with her own.

"What happened, sister? This is a safe place. You can tell me anything."

"We kissed. Jason and I kissed. I kissed him." The words bubbled out of her, extricating themselves and flooding her with relief.

Artemis's eyes widened, although her face remained impassive. "Go on."

"I was trying to jog his happiest memory. I got too close. We were dancing, and I kissed him. He stopped the kiss, thank the goddess. But it happened."

"How did you feel about the kiss?"

Selene's cheeks warmed. She wasn't expecting Artemis to ask her that question. She placed a cool hand to her cheek. "It was pleasant and shocking. Afterward, I knew it was wrong, but when it was happening, it felt like jumping over a waterfall. Exhilarating. Weightless. Almost as if I couldn't stop it if I tried." She rubbed her chest. "And there's more. I feel something here, a tug, like my wolf is drawn to him. Like she's whimpering to be near him."

"Oh dear." Artemis laughed.

"Can you forgive me?" Selene pressed a hand to her chest.

Artemis started. "Forgive you? Whatever for?"

"Men are off-limits to our order."

She tipped her curly gray head. "The encounter ended after the kiss?"

"Yes. But in full disclosure, it was, um, passionate."

"Do you know why we remain celibate here?"

"In honor of the goddess. Our virtue is an offering to her, and in exchange, she gives us power."

Artemis nodded. "Your encounter honored the goddess as well."

Selene blinked rapidly. "Sorry, I'm not following."

"That feeling your wolf is having, you don't recognize

it for what it is? You've been trained to see it in others. Can't you see it in yourself?"

She squeezed her eyes shut. "Jason is my potential mate. Fated by the goddess. If we claim each other, the bond will be blessed by her."

"She does not extend an invitation like that lightly."

Tears formed in her eyes. "Oh, but this isn't how it's supposed to be! I wanted *this* life, here at Sanctuary."

Artemis rubbed her shoulder. "And you can have it if you choose. You kissed him, but you are here and your virtue is intact." She spread her hands. "It is understandable that the experience was confusing to you, but the fact that you told me about it immediately speaks boldly of your character. I am not concerned at all about this incident. You are a very talented spiritual leader, Selene. Add this experience to the many things to come that will help you grow in your faith and abilities." She met her gaze. "If that is what you choose, reject the wolf's bond and stay."

Selene nodded. "Oh, thank you, *Preotka*." She turned back to her bag, feeling light as air. "I should unpack."

"Unless..." Artemis folded her long, graceful arms over her cardigan and narrowed her eyes on Selene.

Selene blinked and turned back toward her mentor.

"Love is a rare and powerful gift. If you genuinely have feelings for Jason, beyond the instincts of your wolf, and he returns those feelings, maybe it's a sign from above that there is a more important role for you in this life than priestess."

Selene gave a breathy laugh. "What could be more important than priestess?"

Artemis didn't miss a beat. "Devoted wife, loving mother, conscientious princess, practitioner of true love. My dear Selene, if you have been blessed with love and a true mate, do not allow it to slip through your fingers. That type of connection is rare, and I fear you'll regret leaving it in your past."

"But how do I know? I have no experience with this. Maybe my feelings are something else. Maybe they won't be returned by him." Selene bit her lip. "Artemis, have you ever... been in love?"

Artemis shook her head. "Only with the pack."

Selene dropped her arms to her sides in frustration and stared at her feet. "This is silly. It was only a kiss. Nothing more."

With a knowing smile, Artemis nodded. "I thought so. But if you do decide it's something more, remember this isn't a prison. You can leave if you want to."

Selene lifted a stack of clothes from her bag and laid them out on the bed. "But there's no coming back if I do."

Artemis cleared her throat. "No. There's no coming back."

TWENTY-ONE

Jason's thoughts refused to stay in the present as he wandered through the garden at Rivergate Manor under a canopy of silvery sunset and slowly emerging stars. He'd tried to stop thinking about Selene and to focus on his business, which was sorely in need of his attention. His scout, Andrew, informed him that the Spackles deal was officially dead because of his neglect. He'd failed miserably. As much as he would have liked to return to business as usual, his mind bounced right back to Selene.

It wasn't just his wolf's innate desire to mark her as his own, although that part was surely there. She was his potential true mate, after all, the bond, even stronger than the one he'd shared with Jessica. That bond seemed to pulse deep within his chest where his wolf still pined for her. His soul and its beast longed to claim that bond, but the truth was, his human heart ached just as badly.

He'd spent the day pacing an empty apartment, remembering how full it felt with her in it. Like a real home.

"Welcome back, brother." Silas broke into Jason's thoughts with a pat on his shoulder as he sidled up next to him. "Selene gave me a glowing review of your willpower and constraint this morning."

Jason adjusted his watch on his wrist, remembering how little restraint he'd shown when he was shoving his tongue down her throat the night before. "It's good to be back," he said mechanically.

"You've certainly put on some weight. Jesus, you're going to pop a button with all the muscle going on under there."

"Funny how a few weeks locked in one's home revives their love of physical activity." Based on his brother's expression, the note of bitterness in his words wasn't lost on Silas.

"It was necessary. I know it wasn't easy, but now you're ready to face Nickelova if she comes for you. That's what's important."

"So when can we try to find her and kill her?"

"After the shift. I've rounded up three wolves, all with military experience. Gerty has agreed to go too. Grateful can't leave her son but has promised to provide magical protection in the form of potions and spells. Do you think you can remember where to go?"

He nodded. "I remember." Jason couldn't wait to destroy the dragon fae who had started all this, made him suffer, only to find true happiness with Selene and experience true suffering all over again when she left. He wanted the dragon bitch to die slowly, but he'd take her death however he could get it. He hoped he was the one to do it, preferably by crushing her heart between his own two hands.

They arrived at the tent where the pack was shedding clothes in preparation for the shift. "See you on the other side of the moon." Silas left him to prepare for the shift.

Jason removed his tailored shirt and pants, toed off his leather loafers, and folded everything in a neat pile in the corner. He left the tent completely naked, his blood bubbling under the surface of his skin. The change was close at hand.

That's when he saw her. Selene locked eyes with him across the sparsely wooded lawn, her beautiful skin gleaming in the moonlight. From the moment he'd met her, he'd admired the way she carried herself, like she lived above the fray, and now was no exception. Her hair was down. Goddess, he loved her hair. The delicate bones of her face added to the long stretch of her body, giving her the look of a ballerina, graceful even in the face of impending pain, an angel in their midst.

The din of the older members of the pack starting to shift filled the space: groans and growls and breaking bones. Jason pitched forward, the tawny fur of his underside breaking out along his abdomen. Human thought was difficult in this state as his wolf mind started taking over, but the last clear thought he had before he changed was a raging need to claim Selene as his. *Mine,* his wolf growled. *Mine.*

And then he surrendered completely to the animal within.

THE NEXT MORNING, LIGHT POURED OVER SELENE'S BODY, heating her skin and creating a pleasant backdrop to the scent of new grass filling her lungs. Spring signified new life. Tiny hatching eggs deep within fresh earth. Budding green things. Blooming moss. Fresh dew. But it was another smell that made her heart twitter—the warm spicy scent of male, musky cloves and chicory, a male whose arm draped across her stomach. *Jason.*

Being this close to him was the stuff of dreams, a world-tilting high that required no drugs or alcohol. With a sleepy grunt, he pulled her tighter against his wide, muscled chest. His hand pressed between her naked breasts, dark hair dappling the thick cords of muscle in his forearm. The contrast between his darker skin and her light sent a current of desire straight to her core.

She shouldn't want him. It was her responsibility to move away.

A werewolf was not responsible for what he or she did in wolf form. It was commonly accepted that a person's wolf had a mind of its own. But lying here in Jason's arms, every second brought her deeper into the realization that it wasn't just her wolf who'd enjoyed Jason's company. As wrong as it might be, she refused to deny herself the pleasure of this moment. It was too perfect. Too good.

They were inside a closely set group of trees, and they were alone. She pretended to be asleep and snuggled in, closing her eyes as the feel of his breath on her hair sent tiny sparks of longing down the length of her neck and across the surface of her skin.

His hand coasted over her nipple, along the flat length of her torso and rounded the curve of her hip. Goddess, it was delectable. A warm ache ignited in her core, her need opening like a flower. She pressed her thighs together against the feeling, suppressing the moan his touch elicited.

She sensed the moment he woke, the realization of her closeness causing his body to tense. He removed his hand from her hip and whispered, "Sorry" into the back of her head. As he rolled away from her, she knew she should act as though she were sorry too, cover up, move away. She should deny that even the blood in her veins was singing for him, delighting in the energy of his touch.

She didn't. She wouldn't lie.

Instead, she rolled onto her back and gazed up at him, naked, vulnerable. He was balanced on his elbow beside her, hovering but not touching. When their eyes locked, her longing was so intense she began to tremble. Tears streamed down her face.

"Oh goddess, I'm so sorry. Did my wolf hurt you? Should I get help?" Jason whispered, his hand floating near her cheek as he studied her.

Selene shook her head and wiped under her eyes. "It's not you or your wolf," she said softly. "It's me. Lying here next to you, I can't pretend anymore."

He swallowed hard, a spark of heat and yearning parading across his features. "Can't pretend what?"

"I can't pretend that I'm not jealous of my wolf." She sobbed quietly. "I wish things were different. I wish I had the freedom to feel what I feel."

He blinked as if her admission sincerely surprised him, then cleared his throat. "What do you feel?"

"I'm falling in love with you, Jason," she admitted, the words tumbling out all at once. "For the first time, I'm questioning what I want for my future. This isn't supposed to happen. I'm supposed to keep a professional distance. But every time I close my eyes, I see you." She turned her head to look away from him. "I'm a terrible person. I've betrayed my role as an acolyte."

A shadow passed over her face, his hand hovering, almost as if he were afraid to touch her. She thought he might pull it away, but then he wiped her tears with his thumb. He stroked along her jaw, encouraging her to face him.

"You're not a terrible person." He shook his head. "Why does this have to be a mistake? Can't you see that I've fallen for you too? I don't care if it's because of the therapy or if we were fated to be together all along. By the goddess, you've gotten under my skin. I felt it, Selene, the moment I saw you. We're potential mates. We have a bond. If you feel the same way, don't we owe it to ourselves to be brave enough to admit it?"

A hot tear escaped the corner of her eye. "It's...complicated. I can't date you. I can't give you time to try us on for size. If I pursue this, there's no going back for me. I'd have to give up my status as an acolyte."

Jason licked his lips. "Oh sweetheart, I'm not suggesting we *try this on for size*. I already know that it fits." He brushed her hair from her forehead. "I'm talking about something exclusive and permanent. I've never had that before. Maybe it won't be easy, but I want it. I want to have it with you." When she couldn't respond immediately around the lump that had formed in her throat, he removed his hand from her face and shifted as though he might get up and walk away.

Goddess help her, she couldn't deny this anymore. Selene reached out and caught him behind the neck. At first he looked surprised. He gripped her wrist, searching her face.

"I want it too," she whispered. "Goddess, I want it too."

A muscle in his jaw twitched. "I've learned to restrain myself around you, but make no mistake, I've wanted you, my wolf has wanted you, since the moment I saw you standing under that tree in Red Grove. You don't know what you do to me. You're playing with fire." His eyes flared amber. His presence loomed like a growing hunger above her. "Do you *know* for sure? Because I do, and I don't think I can resist you anymore."

In answer, she pulled his face toward hers. A rumble came from deep inside his chest, as their mouth's collided, the kiss warm and soft, a question instead of a demand. Her arms snaked around his neck, gripping him tighter. He licked the crease of her lips, an invitation she was more than happy to accept. The erotic feel of his tongue stroking against hers made a rush of heat flare within her. He must have scented her arousal in the air because he inhaled sharply against her lips and stretched out over her, covering her, surrounding her. His elbows landed on either side of her head. His fingers buried in her hair.

It had been so long since she felt desire for any man. She was no virgin but she couldn't ever remember feeling this, this wanting, this fire pooling deep within her. She stroked along his side, delighting in his slightly rougher, warmer skin, up and over the peaks and hollows of his back. She drew him down on her, nails grazing his flesh. He groaned into her mouth.

Breaking away, Jason panted, his chest heaving. "This isn't the right time or place. Not here. Not now." She was surprised that it was Jason who said it. Wasn't she supposed to be the one to protest? "I want it to be special for you. Our first time should be memorable."

Only, she didn't want to wait. She didn't want the opportunity to think or to change her mind. "Please," she said against his lips. She guided his hand to her breast, to her pounding heart.

Amber eyes flashed, a possessive growl vibrating against her chest. Jason's beast had come out to play. He captured her jaw in his hand, stroking along her neck until his hand lightly gripped her throat. Her swallow pressed into his palm. She wasn't afraid. She wanted this. Wanted to be claimed.

Like a long lick of fire, his fingers swept slowly between her breasts, along her abdomen, and sank between her legs.

She gasped when his touch parted her slit, another growl rumbling through him. She was wet, soaking with need, and she moved her hips to strengthen his touch. His thumb began to circle the tangle of nerves at the apex of her thighs as his adept fingers stroked her damp heat. By the time he slid a digit inside and curled his fingers, she was quivering. She arched into him, gasping, needing more. A heady ache had begun low within her, building toward something she desperately wanted.

"I can make you feel good. I want you to feel good," he murmured. He lowered his lips to her stomach, then trailed kisses lower and lower until his lips took over where his thumb had been. At first, her cheeks blazed thinking of him *down there*. After so many years of celibacy, she hadn't expected it. But if her mind held any reservations, the rest of her suppressed that urge as Jason's tongue licked up her center, sending her senses swirling.

She spread her arms on the soft moss and arched her back, pressing harder against his mouth. Needing more. Needing...Two more languid licks and her world expanded into a vision of bright light and intense pleasure. Her inner walls clenched around his fingers, her thighs shaking.

He held her as the aftershocks rocked her body,

lifting his head and licking his lips as if she were the most delicious meal he'd ever had. Rising above her, he stroked her hair back, his hips settling between her legs, with the velvet head of him pressed against her opening, but he hesitated.

"Let's make this real," he gritted out "I don't want shadows or secrecy with you. I want the world to know you're mine. My mate. My wife. My love."

Breathless, she said, "I'll have to step down from my position."

He searched her face, his jaw tightening. A deep breath moved in and out of his lungs. He suddenly looked gravely serious. "I can't ask you to do that. If it's not what you want—"

"You don't have to ask me. I do want to. It's the right thing to do. It's time to make a choice, and I..." She ran her fingers along the back of his ear. "Well, I already have. I choose you, Jason."

The smile he gave her came from a place so deep in his soul she could see his aura in it, as bright spring green as the forest around them.

Until a burly hand clamped down on the back of his neck and lifted him off her in one swift movement. Silas boomed, "What have you done?"

TWENTY-TWO

Jason's back slammed against the nearest tree, Silas holding him there with a stiff forearm to his neck that wasn't nearly as breath-constricting as the guilty lump that had formed in his throat when he realized what he'd been about to do. He'd been about to claim Selene. Selene who was as perfect as she was powerful and deserved someone far better than his sorry ass as a mate.

"Stop!" Selene cried. "He didn't do anything wrong!"

Silas ignored her. "You fucking asshole. Taking advantage of an acolyte! I should beat you senseless for this."

Jason tried to speak, but his windpipe failed under Silas's crushing weight. Even as he bared his teeth, a heaviness deep in his soul made him wonder if his brother was right.

But Selene had a mind of her own and she didn't seem to agree with his self-assessment. She shoved against Silas's massive chest and wedged her waifish body between them. "Silas, I said stop! It wasn't Jason."

Silas turned his focus onto her, his lip curling in disbelief as if a frog in a top hat had started to sing.

"It was me! I initiated it. I'm in love with your brother."

Breath hitching, Jason absorbed that revelation. Selene *loved* him. What happened between them wasn't a mistake. She'd chosen him. This was real.

Jason shoved Silas away from her and swept Selene behind him, his inner wolf so close to the surface it felt like a swarm of bees under his skin. Silas stumbled backward, growling and baring his teeth. *That's right, Brother, I'm strong again.*

"This isn't what you think," Jason snapped. He might find himself unworthy, but he was the one Selene wanted, and he was determined to be the best man he could be for her. Right now, that meant defending her from the unintended consequences of their actions. "Silas," he said sternly, slicing a hand between them. "Just forget you saw anything. It will work itself out soon enough."

Behind him, Selene held up her hands, a wild-eyed panic taking hold. Jason longed to wipe the tears from her eyes, hated that his feelings for her were ripping her apart. He wished he could make it easier for her, but no one could turn back time. He couldn't unlove her, and he wouldn't turn her away if she loved him back.

"Please. Please don't tell anyone. I'm not ready," she

pleaded with Silas. "I will tell Artemis. Give me a chance to tell her myself."

With a shake of his head, Silas seemed to contemplate her words, pacing and cursing to himself. "This... this isn't going to go over well with the pack. How could this happen?"

"Please, Silas." Selene folded her arms over her stomach.

After more grumbling, Silas placed his hands on his hips and let out a deep breath. "You two can't walk back together. People will talk. You"—he pointed at Jason—"go back the long way. Selene, wait five minutes and take the direct route. I don't know what's going on here, but I'll give you the next two days to get your heads on straight. After that, I'll expect action and answers."

Jason glanced at Selene. "Are you going to be okay?"

She nodded once.

"Do you regret—"

"No," she said firmly.

"Now," Silas urged. "I'm not the only one out here, Jason."

With one last lingering gaze at Selene, Jason obeyed his brother and took off at a jog toward Rivergate Manor.

ALONE AMONG THE TREES, SELENE WAITED, HUGGING HERSELF against the cool spring air and the even colder ramifications of her decision to leave Sanctuary and her life as an acolyte. The list she'd started in her head was growing.

She'd have to tell Artemis the truth, move out of Sanctuary, try to find a job and a temporary place to live. Jason would offer to help her, of that she was confident. But she shouldn't presume. Their relationship was too new for that.. Wouldn't it be wrong for her to lean on him too hard, too fast? Perhaps there was a werewolf family in need of a nanny. She'd always been good with children.

As she paced, a high-pitched keening met her ears, the bleat of a dying animal. She wandered toward the sound, peering through a thick web of tree branches. A deer. Mauled by a wolf, by the looks of it. She frowned. It was odd for her kind to kill what it did not eat. Unless... it might have been her or Jason who'd done it, perhaps becoming distracted with each other and not finishing their meal. Well, she couldn't just leave it to suffer. She pushed through the thick line of trees and strode toward the doe, intending to break its neck. But when she reached it, the strangest thing happened. The doe changed. She'd seen it move, watched its throat constrict with its screams. But now it was dead. For some time, by the looks of it. An old, rotting kill. She shook her head. Was she hallucinating from the stress?

"He doesn't mean it," came a woman's voice from behind her.

Selene whirled to face a svelte woman with a platinum-blond bob. Her skin was smooth as marble, and her features as sharp as if they were chiseled from the same. She was wearing a red wrap dress that showed off every curve. But it was the talisman around her neck that gave her away: a twisting dragon with a red stone eye. It looked to be made of pewter, but she knew better. It was dragon scale.

"Nickelova." Selene scanned the line of trees behind the woman in horror. She'd been so caught up thinking about Jason she unwittingly crossed the border of the property and moved beyond the protective enchantment of Rivergate Manor. She hugged herself harder, suddenly feeling more naked than a moment before.

"He's a dog," Nickelova said. "He uses women and throws them away. He used me. Then, when I asked him for help, he dropped me like a hot stone."

"Jason didn't drop you. You tried to kill him and his siblings," Selene said, hoping her words were enough of a distraction that she could make it back to the safety of Rivergate's protections. She inched toward the trees.

"Did he tell you that? It's refreshing to know he speaks of me at all. But it appears I am at a disadvantage. I didn't know about you until today." She frowned. "My curse should have brought Jason to my door by now. When the full moon rose again and he still hadn't come to me, I realized there was a problem. No way could he go this long without sex. Not Jason. Imagine my surprise to track him here only to see him"—she ran a finger along her bottom lip—"with you. Such a tender moment. That sort of thing should have triggered my curse. It seems someone has interfered with my magic. You wouldn't know anything about that, would you?" Her eyebrows knit.

Selene said nothing.

"Did you think I wouldn't suspect anything? Did he

think I wouldn't check on him when he didn't follow my instructions?" Her face contorted, rage turning her elegant features ugly.

Selene darted for the border, running as fast as she could in a wide arc around Nickelova. But one pulse of the dragon fae amulet and her muscles locked in place as rigid as if she'd been turned to stone from the neck down. She cursed.

"What's your name, wolf?"

"Go to hell," Selene said.

The dragon amulet flashed again and Selene's throat constricted. The force at her neck lifted her onto her tiptoes. "Say your name."

"Se... lene...," she rasped, clawing at her throat. The tightening eased, and she dropped to her feet again, pitching forward to take deep, gasping breaths.

"Selene, I think once you get to know me, we are going to be great friends."

"I don't plan to get to know you," Selene said between pants.

"You don't have a choice. I want Jason's help, and I have a feeling that all he needs to see things my way is a little motivation. Judging by what just went on between you two, I think you are exactly what I'm looking for."

Selene screamed as Nickelova's amulet pulsed once more, and an invisible arm snatched her around the waist, doubling her over. All the air whooshed from her lungs, and a rush of darkness overtook her. A moment later, she landed somewhere hard and cold, totally alone.

Jason had just fastened the last button on his dress shirt when he heard Selene's scream, a soul-piercing sound that reached him on a primal level. At a dead run, he navigated the short way back to the place where they'd been. But when he reached the tightly grouped trees, she was gone.

"Selene! Selene!"

"This way." Silas arrived behind him, sniffing the air. The two brothers walked to the tree-lined border of the property and stopped. "She passed beyond the protective boundary."

"Why? Why would she do that?"

"There's a kill." Silas pointed at a dead doe. He approached the carcass, carefully picking his way through the tight web of branches that signified the border. "Do you smell that?"

Jason caught a whiff of someone other than Selene, a dangerous scent he hadn't smelled in weeks. "Fairy magic." A hard lump formed in his throat.

"Fuck." Silas dug his fingers into his wild hair.

Jason's phone rang. He slid it from his pocket, glancing at Silas when he saw who was calling. He tapped the screen and raised it to his ear.

"Jason?" said the familiar, dark voice, edged in gravel. "Ryker from Lost Things."

"This isn't a good time."

"Something just arrived in my store for you."

"What? What are you talking about? Arrived? Did someone bring something in?"

"No, Mr. Flynn. This item appeared where before there was nothing. I think you'd better take a look. I'm sending a picture now."

Jason heard the chirp of a text coming in. One look and he doubled over. "No. No. No."

"It smells of dragon," Ryker said.

"What is it?" Silas asked. "Show me."

Jason held up his phone, his hand trembling so hard he was surprised his brother could make out the picture. But the item was unmistakable. A ponytail of caramel-colored hair lay across the counter at Lost Things, labeled with a simple note. *For Jason Flynn.*

TWENTY-THREE

"Nickelova took Selene." Jason couldn't breathe. This was a living nightmare, the worst possible scenario. He suspected Nickie would come back for *him*. It never once occurred to him that she might target Selene.

Silas grabbed the phone out of Jason's hand. "Who is this guy Ryker? How do we know he's not helping Nickelova?"

"He's a business associate." Jason's voice trembled with a mixture of anger and fear. "Look, Nickie wants me to follow her clues. She's always wanted that. She won't free Selene unless I go to her." Jason strode toward Rivergate.

"You'll be walking right into her trap!" Grabbing his elbow, Silas whirled him around. "She's expecting you to do something rash. She's using Selene as bait."

Jason bit his lip. "And I can't keep her dangling from the hook."

"You'll have to shift again tonight. You'll be vulnerable," Silas said.

"I'll also be at my strongest."

"Until you're not you anymore. The wolf is unpredictable. You could get Selene killed."

"I'll take my chances."

"Wait until after the shift, Jason," Silas said. "Nickelova won't hurt Selene because she needs the hold over you. It'll give us time to prepare."

"I am not going to leave Selene in the clutches of that madwoman a moment longer than I have to."

"You can't do this alone."

"I can't wait for the others." Jason shook his head and pulled his elbow from Silas's grip.

"Just... give me until tonight." Silas strode quickly, side by side with Jason. "Let me talk to Gerty and Grateful. I'll put together a team."

Jason ground his teeth.

"Promise me you'll wait. Just until tonight. Until we have a plan." Silas was asking for his trust. His brother had earned that much. And his logic was sound.

Jason nodded. "What other choice do I have?"

Silas paused and pulled Jason into a hug. "We're going to get her back, brother."

"Right." Jason parted ways with Silas, heading for the parking lot while his brother took off toward Rivergate Manor. Thank the goddess his brother hadn't given him a direct alpha command. He hated to lie, but when it came to Selene, Jason was singularly focused. "Sorry, brother, but I made this mess—now I intend to clean it up."

"Do you have anything in this hoarder's dream of a shop that can kill a dragon fae?" Jason asked Ryker. Selene's ponytail was draped across his hands, her soft hair a gauntlet thrown at his feet. At least there was no blood. Nickelova could have left her entire head. No, this invitation was also a promise she was still alive, although he assumed that assurance had a time limit.

"Many things in my shop could be used as tools capable of killing a dragon fae, but wielding them is another matter entirely. All work in the same way. The fairy is immortal until you cut out her heart."

"A sword or a dagger then?" Jason perused the stacks of dusty artifacts around him. "One that won't try to kill me like that ring you sold me."

Ryker's dark eyes flashed. "I warned you about the ring. You wouldn't listen."

Jason nodded. "Yes, yes, you warned me. Excuse me for being moody. A fae psychopath has my girlfriend, Ryker. I need help and I need it fast."

"I thought I recognized this as Selene's," Ryker said, stroking the hair. Jason yanked the ponytail away from his fingers. "Pity. I liked the girl. She had pluck."

"So find something to help me rescue her."

Ryker's tattoo glowed and his eyes flashed with red fire.

He scanned the stacks of seemingly unorganized artifacts. Blowing like a dark wind through the narrow aisles, he stopped at a shelf and selected a short silver rod. "Try this."

Careful not to touch anything, Jason navigated the stacks and caught up to Ryker. "What is it?" He gingerly lifted the cylinder between his thumb and forefinger like it might explode in his hand at any moment. The metal baton was about four inches long with a one-inch diameter. Aside from possibly being used to bludgeon Nickelova, he couldn't think why the item would be useful at all.

"Well? Give it some intent," Ryker said. "And your full grip." He tucked the cylinder into Jason's palm and squeezed.

Reflexively, Jason raised the hand holding the silver cylinder, withdrawing from Ryker's tight grip. Jagged blades emerged from each end, thin and razor sharp, with a metal-on-metal clang that resounded through the store. Jason laughed and loosened his grip. The blades retracted into the weapon.

"That's better," Ryker said. "This is the bladed staff of Ocebel, the ancient siren goddess. It will react to your intent and increase the speed and accuracy of your strikes when near water. Water magic is a counterbalance to fire magic. You'll find this helpful in more ways than one. I recommend bringing some of the wet stuff with you."

"So I cut out her heart and that will kill her?"

Ryker laughed. "No. Removing her heart will make her mortal and give you power over her." He floated between the stacks, his body going misty at the edges. "Once you have her heart, you can kill the fae if you so choose or manipulate her to do your will. The heart itself has magical properties even if the fae is deceased, but keeping her alive and holding her heart will make her your slave."

"So I remove her heart." Jason rolled the cylinder in his palm. "And then I can kill her. Sounds easy enough."

Ryker laughed. "You do know that dragon fae can shift into actual dragons at will, don't you? They aren't dragons, but her fairy magic can transfigure her into the beast when provoked. Although she'll avoid that transformation if she can. It will drain her energy and cost her human logic."

"Like a werewolf," Jason muttered. "She won't have her higher faculties?"

"Exactly. If she transforms, she must rely on the instincts of the dragon she becomes. Not ideal in all situations. But make no mistake, those instincts will protect her heart with three tons of scaled muscle, razor-sharp teeth, and a barbed tail."

"Why can't anything be easy?" Jason activated the bladed staff again, testing its weight in his hand.

Ryker stroked his hairless chin and stared at him for a moment. "No offense, but playing the hero isn't exactly your modus operandi. This girl must be special."

Jason locked eyes with the demon. "She is. Saved-my-life, keep-her-forever special."

"I was surprised how eagerly she risked her life to find you the night she came to me."

"Thanks for looking out for her."

"It wasn't easy." He licked his lips. "Selene is a temptation for the senses."

Jason growled, turning one of the blades of the cylinder toward the demon.

"Relax, my friend. I know better than to bite the hand that feeds me."

Jason released his grip and the silver rod returned to its original state. "I assume I can borrow this on credit and return it when I'm finished. Or do you want payment upfront?"

"You can borrow it, for free, on one condition." Ryker's eyes filled with ruby fire. "As I mentioned, a dragon fae's heart has magical properties that a demon in my line of business would find exceptionally useful. Bring me the heart, and we'll call it even."

One of the skills Jason possessed that made him an excellent investor was his ability to read people. Ryker was a demon, but his intentions weren't evil. Self-serving, perhaps, but the guy had a moral code. His word was good, and most of the time, he spoke the truth.

"It's a deal," Jason said.

The demon tipped his head in affirmation. "Good luck, Jason Flynn. I certainly hope to see you, Selene, and the dragon's heart in my shop very soon."

Jason nodded and made his way out of Lost Things. There was much to do, and this was only his first stop.

When Jason arrived at the Route 9 bridge over Eagle River, he wasn't sure what he expected. Not a blinking neon sign that said *dragon this way,* but something, some clue that he was headed in the right direction. The picture Nickelova had implanted in his brain showed two mountains in the distance, beyond the forest he was looking at now. Only, standing here, with the road, the river, and everything else as pictured, the mountains were conspicuously absent. He took this as a sign. He would hike toward where the mountains should have been and trust that the way would reveal itself when he got close enough.

He tied the laces of his new hiking boots and donned the backpack of camping supplies he'd packed, checking that the silver cylinder was strapped to the side and well within reach. Then he sent Silas three texts. The first was a picture of his Bugatti in front of the Route 9 sign he'd told him about. The second was a picture of the place where the mountains should be. The third contained two simple words: "I'm sorry."

His phone rang almost immediately after he hit Send, but he didn't answer. He couldn't risk Silas giving him a direct alpha command to return to Rivergate. He needed to do this, and if he didn't go now, he might lose his nerve.

His brother was right. He was probably walking into a trap. That was semiobvious. But without a doubt, Jason couldn't live with himself another minute knowing she was there and he was here. He'd happily go to his death or to his slavery to save Selene. Silas would never let him do that though. His brother didn't realize life meant nothing to Jason without her. She was his mate, true and simple. He had to do this.

He turned off the phone and tossed it into his backpack. And then there was nothing but his boots and a narrow footpath that seemed to lead in the direction Nickelova wanted him to go.

SELENE SHIVERED IN THE DARKNESS, HER HANDS GROPING THE stone floor beneath her. What had Nickelova done to her? One minute they were standing just outside the bounds of Rivergate, and then she was here. It all seemed to happen in the blink of an eye. Only Selene had the oddest notion that she'd been unconscious for some time. The cold breeze on her neck seemed to confirm that hypothesis. Her hair was missing, cut short at her nape. When had that happened?

"Hello?" she called through a dry throat.

A fire blazed to life in an alcove of stone nearby, flooding the room with light. As her eyes adjusted, she took in the vast cavern around her. She was not alone.

"Welcome back from la-la land." Nickelova's high-heeled black boots click-clacked against the stone floor as she approached Selene. Stalagmites and stalactites broke the otherwise normal continuity of the room, which included a red Persian carpet and a plush-looking sofa near the fireplace.

Nickelova's posh appearance intimidated Selene. Her

sleek platinum bob and tall, lanky build were something she associated with runway models, as was the red dress that wrapped around her body in a way that revealed plenty of cleavage and leg. But it was the dragon-scale amulet that hung from her neck that unsettled Selene the most. It throbbed with power as she neared and seemed to infuse Nickelova with a toxic confidence.

"Jason won't come for me," Selene blurted. "I'm just an acolyte priestess who acted as his spiritual advisor. My life is not worth risking a member of the royal family."

"Hmm. Why do women like you constantly underestimate yourselves? You barely brush your hair, throw on any old rag that will cover you, and then creep around like a little mouse trying your best to be invisible. But clearly you are not invisible, Selene. The affection I witnessed Jason showing you was unusual for the man. For any man actually. So, little mouse, it seems you've been noticed despite your best efforts."

Cheeks warming, Selene lowered her eyes. "I think you read more into it than there was."

Nickelova rolled her eyes. "Let me enlighten you. The curse I placed on Jason's vice was meant to force him to come to me. Obviously someone broke that curse. But part of my magic remains. A spell I placed on him long ago, on the evening we first met. You might call it a tracking device. It's how I found him and possessed that woman he was with in the first place. When he gets busy, I feel what he feels... I see what he sees. But oddly, I hadn't felt the tug of my curse in weeks. When I felt his *interaction* with you this morning, I went to him immediately, well, as close as I could get to the protective enchantment. I didn't just happen upon your rendezvous, Selene. In a way, I was watching you from the inside out. News flash: Jason loves you, little mouse." She said the last part through her teeth. "Let's stop pretending he doesn't. It wastes both our time."

Selene sputtered unintelligibly, trying her best to find the right words of denial, but Nickelova continued.

"I can't say I'm not jealous. I had hoped that *I* could be the one to master Jason's heart. But accommodations must be made. You will have to be the carrot on the stick. It's why I've kept you alive." Nickelova smiled wickedly, her eyes shifting to focus on something behind Selene.

Selene turned tentatively, only to let out a piercing scream. She was standing in front of a pile of bones. Human, animal, all mixed together in a grisly pile of death. Some were bleached, some burned, and some had bits of flesh still clinging to them.

Hand clasped over her mouth and nose, she backed toward Nickelova, only to bump into a wall where there was no wall. After a frantic inspection of the area, she accepted the truth. She was a prisoner, jailed with a pile of bones behind an invisible barrier.

"No need for hysterics," Nickelova said. "A girl's gotta eat."

Selene turned from the bones and swallowed the bile rising in her throat. She was still naked, but at least the fire Nickelova had started warmed the cave to a temperature that stalled her shivering.

"Why Jason? I thought you were helping Alex overthrow the Fireborn clan. Shouldn't you be after Silas? He's the alpha."

"Woman to woman?" Nickelova paced toward her, all fire and shadows. "Alex turned out to be a disappointment. See for yourself." She turned her body and pointed at the far wall of the cavern. Alex Ravien Bloodright was suspended like a specimen in a jar, embedded behind another invisible barrier in the rocky wall. His eyes were closed, and his hair and limbs floated in reddish fluid. "He's healing," Nickelova said, "but slowly. He would have died weeks ago if not for my near-constant presence and the fire lily juice I stole from the fae hospital."

In her studies as an acolyte, Selene had read that dragon fae were once hunted almost to extinction for the power of their hearts. There was a reason Nickelova had stayed close to Alex in this cave, why she'd relied on her curse on Jason for information instead of the direct approach. The proximity of her heart was healing Alex, perhaps keeping him alive. Fairy hearts could be used in the most dangerous of spells, even to raise the dead, according to certain holy texts. Nickelova was keeping Alex alive, but at what cost? If Alex was conscious at all, his state of being was horrific.

"Alex is too weak to do much more than sleep just now. When I wake him, he'll need someone strong to help us achieve our goals. We'll never take down Silas and rule the Lycanthropic Society without help."

"You don't want to kill Jason—you want him to join you." Selene shook her head. "You can't truly believe that will ever happen. He will never help you overthrow the council. He'd die before he'd betray the pack."

Turning toward the fire, Nickelova hugged herself, rubbing her outer arms. "He will... now that I have you. He's already on his way. I'll have him tamed in the amount of time it takes me to show him his dear, sweet Selene, dirty and shivering in my prison."

"You're wrong."

"The wolf in him won't be able to stand it, little mouse. The more enthusiastically he bows to me, the better your living conditions will get."

"No." Selene tucked her chin, her eyes burning. Why had she been so stupid? If she'd stayed away from Jason and maintained her vows as she should have, none of this would have ever happened.

"Don't fret. You both have the opportunity to be on the right side of history. When Alex and I rule the supernatural world, you'll be free to finally be your true self. For too long we've been forced into an existence based on balance and harmony."

"That is the law of the goddess," Selene said. "We must maintain balance, or the world will fall into darkness and chaos."

"Some of us could do with a little darkness," she snapped. "What has the goddess ever done for me?"

Selene furrowed her brow. Saying Nickelova was crazy was an understatement. "The goddess, Hecate, created all supernatural beings."

Nickelova scoffed. "But the horned god, Panaal, is the source of much of their power. The power of fire. The power of chaos. Hecate and Panaal collaborated to design the reality we currently live in, rules and regulations based on a balance between the masculine and feminine. But Hecate is a wicked goddess. There is no balance. Demons and vampires live in the shadows. Dragons are almost extinct and with them the dragon fae like me whose powers are born from a relationship with them." She twirled the amulet between her fingers. "When a fairy and a wolf rule the supernatural world, we'll change everything. We'll remake everything under Panaal's eye."

Selene shuddered to think how the world might change under the rule of Nickelova and Alex. Humans would likely be hunted to extinction. Or farmed by vampires. Werewolf children, human until their first shift, might become vampire targets, setting the two species at odds. The most powerful witches, the demigoddesses known as Hecate, would be overwhelmed with their charge of maintaining balance and the management of their Hellmouth prisons. What Nickelova wanted would completely change life as they knew it. She had to be stopped.

"You're mad. If what you're saying is true, you'd unleash the underworld."

Nickelova sighed. "That, little mouse, is the idea. Now you'd better get some rest. Jason is on his way. You want to be strong enough to watch me break him, don't you?"

TWENTY-FOUR

As the sun began to sink over the dense woods, Jason calculated he'd traveled about fifteen miles in the direction of the nonexistent mountains. He hadn't found a portal or any directions from Nickelova on how to reach her. Still, he was confident the dragon fae knew he was coming. Her Spidey-Sense was powerful enough to detect when a fly entered her web.

Jason was no fool. He didn't labor under the delusion that he could sneak up on Nickelova's lair. On the contrary, he assumed he'd be invited in. That was the point, wasn't it? Once inside, he'd lie, cheat, beg, or steal to get Selene out alive. Then Nickelova could do with him what she would.

When he came upon a stream, he made camp, thankful for the fresh water and a safe, stony bank to start a fire. He pulled the chains and locks from his backpack. He wouldn't need a tent. In less than an hour he'd shift into wolf form and grow his own fur coat. All he had to do was keep the wolf contained until morning.

As the fire blazed to life and he put a kettle of water on to prepare his freeze-dried meal, he undressed and crisscrossed the chains around his neck and chest. When he was confident the wolf would not be able to free itself, he padlocked himself to the nearest tree. No need to hide the key. Paws weren't good at using one.

He huddled inside his bedroll and ate four human helpings of the food he brought. As the sun dipped below the horizon and a full round moon came into view, he wondered what Nickelova was doing to Selene. Was she cold? In a place she could safely shift? Had she been fed? Clothed? The thought of her being tortured because of him made his stomach turn.

"Don't you hurt her," he yelled toward the place where the mountains should be. "Don't you hurt her, Nickie!"

When his skin began to tingle and his bones to stretch, he used his last human strength to douse the flames of his campsite. No sense risking a forest fire. Once he sprouted fur, he wouldn't need the extra warmth.

His groan turned into a growl as the pull of the moon took over. And the person who was Jason gave way to the wolf within.

THE FIRST THING JASON NOTICED WHEN HE WOKE THE NEXT morning was the temperature. It was considerably colder than before he'd shifted. The second thing was the snowstorm. It swirled around him, stinging his skin and catching in his eyelashes as he blinked toward the risen sun. He trembled, naked, in a wolf-sized dent of packed snow.

Fuck! The chains were gone and so was his campsite. He stood and turned in a circle but could barely see through the wild white blizzard around him. What he could make out, as he hugged his naked chest, was that he'd awakened on the side of a mountain, and a thousand meters or more above him was the mouth of a cave.

He cursed again as he realized all his gear, the silver cylinder Ryker had lent him, his phone, his clothes, everything he'd brought with him was back at the campsite, wherever that was. It seemed his wolf had escaped the chains and found the portal without him. Or else had been freed intentionally. He was betting the second. Nickelova wanted him weak. It was possible she wanted him dead.

Shivering, Jason began the painful climb toward the cave, teeth chattering in the storm. If he was lucky enough to make it there before freezing to death, he prayed the goddess would send him some ideas, because he had nothing to fight Nickelova with, aside from a lovesick heart and his two bare hands.

Reaching for a stone, he pulled himself up the eversteepening side of the rock. His fingers and toes were bright red and hurt like a bitch. The pain in his extremities told him he was in trouble. Frostbite, for sure.

Bad turned to worse as he neared the mouth of the cave. He lost all feeling in his hands and feet, the tips of his fingers blackening. Not only could he no longer grip the side of the mountain, but severe fatigue had set in, tempting him to curl up and fall asleep, a choice that would surely mean his death. Close but not close enough. It was hopeless. His body could go no farther. As the cold and the wind coaxed him toward unconsciousness, he closed his eyes and tried to meditate as Selene had taught him, to escape the pain by retreating to a place within his own head.

And then she was there, the bright blue light of Selene's soul on that plane of consciousness where they'd met before. "It's a trap," she said. "Nickelova is coming for you."

Was it real? Or a figment of his desperate imagination. Darkness closed in on him. He stopped fighting.

"I love you," he murmured. "And I'm sorry."

"Wake up, sleepyhead," Nickelova jeered. "You're no good to me dead."

Jason's body slapped the floor in front of a raging fire. He might have screamed if he had any control over his body at all. Unfortunately, that was not the case. He was conscious and in pain but physically immobile.

"Your wolf surprised me. After I freed him, he made it

all the way to the vertical drop outside my cave before giving up. Much farther than I expected. Still, you are exactly in the state I hoped you'd be in when you arrived."

Slowly, painfully, Jason blinked his eyes, his warming limbs throbbing with pain.

Nickelova held a small vial over his lips. "A drop of fire lily juice can heal you, but before I give it to you, I need you to see who I have here with me." She yanked his chin to the side so he was facing a large pile of bones near the back of the cave.

Standing naked, her dirt-marred flesh shivering, Selene pressed her hands against an invisible barrier between them. Her butchered hair curled around her ears, rough-cut and matted. Jason tried to speak, tried to move to her, but he couldn't. His words were useless grunts.

"There, there, lover boy. We can talk about what happens to her next when you're better. It's all up to you. You decide her fate. But mark my words, if you betray my trust, it won't be you freezing to death outside my cave. It will be her."

With that, Nickelova tilted Jason's head back and administered a drop of healing elixir.

Warmth radiated from his stomach out to his extremities, thawing his frozen fingers and toes and returning the blackening flesh to a ruddy hue. The process was painful, like burning from the inside out, but Jason welcomed the pain. He channeled every ounce of suffering into the dark place in his soul, the place he planned to draw on when he had the opportunity to rip Nickelova's heart out.

As the pain reached a crescendo, Jason's muscles spasmed. He curled on his side, his eyes catching on a glowing column of liquid entrenched in the stone wall on the far side of the cave. *What the hell?* Alex! He was naked, suspended inside like some sort of science experiment gone wrong. Eyes open, unblinking, he stared at Jason. Was he dead? Preserved? His body appeared to be healed. Why was Nickelova keeping him in that state?

Jason grunted and lifted a knuckle in Alex's direction.

"Oh, you found Alex. He's almost ready to return to us. Your sister's attack left him very near death, but I suspended him there, lung torn, liver split. He would have died without my intervention. That's fire lily balm he's encased in. It's healed him from the inside out. I could revive him now, but I want to leave him where he is until you and I have a chance to... reconnect. Alex can be difficult. Jealous."

Stretching and contracting his hands, Jason tested his major muscle groups, rolling his neck as his body finished healing. He swallowed. Cleared his throat.

"I'm here now." Jason locked eyes with the beast in the red dress. "Let the girl go."

Nickelova gave a breathy chuckle, the edges of her pale hair catching in her sticky red lipstick as she leaned over him. "I can't let that happen. I need your loyalty and fidelity, Jason, and she's my leverage to make sure I get it."

Although everything inside him wanted to turn

toward Selene, to swear his love and loyalty to her, he knew doing so would seal her fate. Her survival and his mission's success depended on convincing Nickelova to underestimate his feelings for Selene and to lower her guard. To trust him.

He was naked, weaponless, in the heart of the fairy's lair. But Selene had taught him that his soul was composed of great darkness as well as extraordinary light. He'd worked hard to get back to the light, to be good enough for Selene. But just now? This was a job for the darkness. He reached deep, calling up memories of Professor Matthews, of the dark days that once ruled his soul. Internally, he whistled for his wolf, loosed the vice he'd worked so hard the past month to suppress. Then he shielded his heart and did what he knew he had to do.

Composing himself, Jason rose to his feet, turning away from Alex to face Nickelova. Thank the goddess his back was to Selene. He wasn't sure he could do this if he could see her. He allowed his gaze to rake down Nickelova's face, linger on her breasts, her waist, and come to rest at the apex of her thighs. With some effort, he lifted one corner of his mouth, flashing the roguish smile he'd perfected over the years. He lowered his chin and peered at her through thick lashes.

"Why do you feel like you need her?" Jason said. "Haven't I always been a good doggie and come when you called?"

"Don't play me for the fool. I know what you feel for this girl. I felt it through our connection. Magic doesn't lie," Nickelova said through her teeth.

Jason approached her as he ran his gaze over her again. Closer, until his lips hovered next to hers and the back of his knuckles skimmed the front of her dress. "If your curse is so good at reading my feelings, tell me Nickelova, what am I feeling now?"

He almost cheered when he saw her lips part on an inhale and her thighs press together against the ache he presumed he'd started there. Before Jason had known what she was, he'd been a thorough and careful lover to Nickelova. He'd made her beg and scream. He prayed to the goddess that the catnip he'd planted was enough to lure her back.

"Hmmm." She looked down between them at Jason's naked body. "Is that for me?"

"Why don't you get a better look and find out?" he whispered. "And once you get a good look, you better taste it to see if it's your flavor."

She narrowed her eyes on him.

"I've missed you, Nickie." Jason pressed his lips to hers, the sticky feel of her lipstick smearing across his mouth. He forced himself to ignore the repulsion growing within him. He'd faked this before, and he'd do it again if it meant Selene's life. He kissed Nickelova as if Selene's life depended on it, grabbed her hips, and ground himself into her belly.

Breaking the kiss, she panted, breathless, between them. "I knew you couldn't deny what we had together forever. You are more than simply a werewolf prince, Jason. You deserve to be alpha." She trailed her fingers under one of his nipples and down the hills and valleys of his abdomen. "When Alex wakes, you'll defeat him, force him to bow to you, then the three of us will take your pack and your society. And you will be alpha."

"You think *I* should call the shots instead of Alex?" That genuinely surprised him until he thought about Alex's body in the jar. Alive or not, healed or not, he was obviously not the man he used to be. His body was likely weak after months of lack of movement, and who knew what kind of damage being jarred like a preserved frog might have done to his brain? He finally understood why Nickelova had wanted him here so badly. She needed him. There was no telling how much Alex there was left.

"Oh, I think you can rise to the occasion, and with my help, you'll have more power than you ever dreamed." She licked her lips.

"First things first," Jason said. "Where can we be alone? I want to show you how I reconnect."

"Right here isn't good enough for you?"

"There's no bed."

"You've never needed a bed before."

He sighed. "I don't like the audience."

"Afraid to upset the girl?" Nickelova asked with venom in her voice.

Jason forced himself not to look in Selene's direction and instead turned his gaze on Alex. "Actually, I was referring to your boyfriend. The way his eyes are open like he's watching us... It's creepy."

Nickelova frowned. "Hmm. He'll have to get used to the idea. No time like the present."

Jason cringed. "Are you telling me he's awake in there? He can see us?"

"And hear us. He's in an altered state of consciousness, but his senses still work. Everything is simply slowed down."

With a shake of his head, Jason tried to maintain his composure. He called on the wolf again, who growled and eyed his prey. "Privacy, Nickelova. Now!"

He was taking a risk speaking to her like that. He was defenseless, and she could shred him with one pulse of her amulet. But he'd had enough experience with her to know she liked a man to take control. Nickelova was a fairy, but she was also all female. And Jason wasn't above using sex as a weapon. He stared her down.

"Come, my darling." She threaded her fingers into his and led him past Selene's cell. Jason glanced at her, just long enough to notice Selene's tearstained face. He prayed to a goddess he didn't believe in that she'd catch on to what he was doing. *Trust me*, he thought. But there was no way to tell her. Nickelova turned a corner, and they descended deeper into the mountain.

TWENTY-FIVE

Selene wiped under her eyes. Had Jason just tried to send her a message? *Trust me.* The phrase had popped into her head. More likely it was a fabrication by her subconscious to try to convince her there was a reason for this nightmare.

When Jason had ignored her and approached Nickelova, she'd been devastated. Watching him kiss her had almost ripped her heart out. She didn't want to believe that Jason would turn on her so quickly, but she'd seen the darkness in him and knew what he was capable of. Jason and Nickelova had a history, a history that might be repeating itself.

The way Jason had looked at Nickelova was the same haunting way he'd looked at her that first day in his apartment and the time he'd almost lost control and she'd had to use her power against him. It was his wolf, his vice, back again from the graveyard of his past. Her first instinct was to believe he'd lost control.

But the more she thought about it, the more she wondered if Jason had more power over his wolf than she was giving him credit for. He'd arrived naked and alone. All he had at his disposal was his cunning, and his most practiced weapon within that arsenal was his ability to seduce. Was he truly attracted to Nickelova, or was he drawing her in, trying to earn her trust?

Her breathing slowed. Her tears dried. Of course that was it. Her mate was too smart and too savvy for this to be anything else. He'd found a way to lure Nickelova from the room, which meant she was alone. Alone for the first time since she'd been imprisoned here. Whirling, she scanned the pile of bones, looking for the sharpest one she could find. As she lifted it from the pile, she made a choice. She wouldn't think about or analyze what was going on wherever Nickelova had taken Jason. Instead, she'd devote all her mental power to finding a way out. Today she would not play the victim. Selene was a survivor.

Dragging the bone along the wall, she tested the confines of the space she was in. Three stone walls capped by a magical force that seemed impenetrable. But as Selene inspected the place where the magic met the stone, she found an irregularity in the surface. Digging her finger into the small opening, she was able to extend past the magical barrier. She picked up the bone and wedged the point into the hole, dislodging a chunk of rock the size of a fist.

As she brushed the rubble away and repositioned her tool, her gaze landed on Alex in his glowing ruby tomb.

His eyes were staring directly at her. Were they like that before? She'd recalled his eyes being closed. How much could he see from there? How aware was he?

Selene decided it didn't matter. For now, he wasn't a threat, and she had her work cut out for her.

TWENTY-SIX

As inconspicuously as possible, Jason swept his gaze around the room where Nickelova led him, looking for anything sharp he could use to pry her heart out of her chest. A large bed at the center of the room was dressed in oxblood linens. The lacquered black furniture, including a dresser and nightstand unfortunately provided no hardware he could break off and stab her with. Neither did the gold crane print dressing screen that divided the room.

"You must love red and black," he said.

"It's more than a preference. Red and black are the colors of my bloodline. They may not mean anything to you, but to me and my six siblings, they are the colors of home."

"Six?"

"Brothers. Dragon Fae always birth seven young. Females are rare. It's why there are so few of us."

"What do your brothers think of your plan to shack up with a werewolf and rule the world?"

She scoffed. "They don't understand. So few are evolved enough to look beyond their lineage." She rolled her shoulders back. "I don't want to talk about my family."

She scanned his naked body. He was still smudged with dirt and blood from his failed attempt to climb the mountain. "You need a bath," she said. With a pulse of her amulet, a tub of hot water appeared behind him.

Water. Ryker had mentioned it weakened fire magic, and dragon fae magic leveraged the element of fire. Jason hoped the demon was right. He stepped into the tub and lowered himself under the surface, mind racing. He needed a plan. *Think.*

She sat down on the upholstered bench at the end of the bed and crossed her legs, her spiky heel bobbing. "Now tell me, Jason, why didn't you come to me sooner?" Her voice was loaded with cynicism.

Jason grabbed the soap and started scrubbing his chest, his arms, in an effort to buy time. A lie. He needed a lie, and it better be a good one. "Silas's friend is a witch. She detected your curse and broke it. After that, Silas locked me up. I've been on house arrest until now."

"Lies. You came for the girl. I know you did," Nickelova said.

"I was using the girl. I came for you."

"Liar."

Flashing a practiced smile, he looked directly at her and moved his hands lower, between his legs. "You don't think I'm here for you?" One thing about Nickelova, her personality was predictably narcissistic. She would prefer to believe he was there for her, undoubtedly hold herself above a woman like Selene, and he planned to use that to his advantage.

She tipped her head back slightly, her lips parting, her nipples pearling behind the red material of her dress. Her eyes focused on the place where he touched himself beneath the water.

"We had some good times, didn't we, Nickie? Those nights at Hunt Club?"

She uncrossed and recrossed her legs, her cheeks coloring.

"You could join me," he drawled. "I could use some help in here."

She rose from her seat and crouched behind the tub, her arms slipping around his neck from behind. "You'd better not be toying with me, Jason Flynn. I won't be as forgiving next time."

He grabbed her forearm. "Next time? So you forgive me?"

Leaning over his shoulder, she laid a violent kiss on his mouth in response. He tried to block out the disgust he was feeling as he ran his hand around the back of her neck, under the guise of reaching for her zipper.

"Mmm," she moaned. "Do you want this body, Jason?"

"Not just your body, Nickie. I want your heart." He yanked the amulet over her head in one lithe move, tearing out a clump of her hair in his haste, then flipped her over his shoulder and into the bath, shoving her by the neck to the bottom of the tub. By the time she broke the surface, he was across the room. He looped the amulet around his own neck. Now that he'd neutralized her magic, all he needed to do was break her neck and cut out her heart. He scanned the room franticly for something to use.

"You fucking bastard," she shrieked, scrambling to claw her way out of the tub. She wasn't graceful about it, and he thanked Ryker for the tip about the water. "The amulet is useless unless I give you the fairy power and knowledge to wield it."

"I figured as much, but I'm more interested in keeping it from you than using it myself." He crouched, hands raised between them, ready to kill her with his bare hands. "If you're going to take me down, you're going to have to do it without magic."

Nickelova broke out in peals of laughter. "You fucking idiot. Do you know where the power of the amulet comes from? Dragon scale. And while I need it in my human form, scales are something dragon fae have all on our own."

As if she'd been hit by an axe, her skin split and her blood sprayed toward him only to be sucked back toward her shifting body. Gruesome round segments transformed into scales. She grew and changed in the most violent and grotesque transition he'd ever seen in a shifter. But as terrifying as the transition was, the end result almost knocked him on his ass.

A full-sized adult dragon hissed at him as he stumbled backward out the door, terror gripping his chest and squeezing the air from his lungs. She was bigger, deadlier in this form than he'd ever imagined. Her razor-sharp teeth gnashed in his direction. No wonder her family colors were red and black. Her scales glinted like blood-stained obsidian.

Scrambling out the door, he tore through the winding tunnel that led to the main chamber, thankful for his superhuman werewolf speed. The only advantage he had was the natural design of the passageway, which was narrow enough to slow the dragon down. It also served to partially conceal him from her slashing teeth.

A whoosh like a fireplace bellow came from behind him. *Oh shit!* He sprinted faster. Fire, hot and blazing, sprayed against the wall behind him, singeing his back. When he emerged into the main chamber, he dodged behind a large stalagmite and desperately searched for something to use as a weapon.

"Jason!" Selene called.

He searched behind the invisible force field that capped her cell, finally finding her tucked into the far corner of the alcove. She'd chiseled a hole the size of her head in the section of stone at the far edge. "I'm sorry," he yelled. "I love you, Selene. It was the only thing I could think of." He pointed to the amulet hanging uselessly around his neck.

Nickelova turned the corner, her claws clicking on the stone, sounding eerily similar to the click-clack of her high heels.

"Crap, she's big," Selene muttered, eyes wide.

"And breathes fire," Jason whispered back. "Got any ideas?"

The tapping claws stopped, and the rushing of air started again. Jason pulled his shoulders in, trying to make himself as small as possible behind the stone formation.

Selene's gaze darted to the dragon and back to Jason. "Catch." She tossed a long, sharp bone through the hole. It skidded to a stop near his feet. He bent over to pick it up only to abandon that idea when fire blasted between them.

Head tucked under his arms, Jason avoided the worst of the flames, but still the smell of burning hair had him slapping out a spark near his temple.

"She stops moving when she blows," Selene said. "She's like a statue."

So that's what had given him the head start earlier. His werewolf speed was only part of his advantage. When she'd tried to fry him in the corridor, she'd had to stop to do so.

The flames abated, and the clicking talons resumed. Selene jumped out from behind the stone and clapped her hands. "Hey you, hot mess! Yeah you, bitch. Over here!" She waved her hands. The dragon roared, advancing on Selene.

Jason rushed from his hiding place, sweeping the bone into his hand and skidding across the floor under the dragon. The dirt and grit bloodied his hip. He looked up from his place between her legs, the dragon huffing in air again, her chest glowing crimson as she readied another blast of flames. With all his strength, he thrust the bone between the scales along her breast.

And failed at breaking her skin.

A single scale popped off her torso and clattered beside him. The dragon, otherwise impervious to the sharp length of bone, bellowed a *Jurassic Park* worthy roar that reverberated through the cavern. He stabbed twice in the exposed spot, horrified when the point bounced off the leathery skin. The dragon turned a tight circle, trying to reposition its slashing jaws to reach him.

"Hey!" Selene yelled, tossing another bone through the hole she'd made in her cell. It was enough to distract the dragon for a split second, long enough for Jason to race from between its legs and around the room. There was no good place to hide, but he flattened himself against the wall beside Alex's glass coffin.

Selene held up a meaty, rotting bone. "Come on. You want a snack? Come and get me!"

Nickelova struck at Selene, her snout bouncing off her own magical barrier. Jason's eyebrows shot up. Nickelova's dragon was not unlike his wolf. She was in there, for sure, but she didn't have the same human consciousness.

Selene waved the bone while the dragon scratched against her own magic, then sniffed the edges of Selene's cell, finding the hole she'd chiseled. *Shit!* The dragon dug its talons in, scratching and scraping at the opening until its snout could almost fit through the damn thing. If Jason didn't do something, Selene's might be the next set of bones on the pile.

Jason looked at the amulet around his neck, trying to will it to work. Nothing. He was on his own. "Hey, bitch! Anyone tell you that red makes you look bloated?" He waved his bone at the dragon. It worked. She turned from her Selene-under-glass dinner and stalked toward him, her wings flattening against her back.

Nickelova's reptile eyes locked on Jason and she froze. He watched her neck undulate with rapid swallows, the space around her heart reddening with heat.

"Fuck me!" Jason ducked and ran just as the fire rained against the wall he'd been pressed against. Red heat swallowed Alex's suspended body. From Jason's vantage point, he could see the dragon fire cause a sharp crack in the barrier containing him. The break spread, the sound of cracking glass barely audible above the roaring flames. Nickelova closed her mouth, extinguishing the fire, just as the fracture reached the top of the barrier. With a snap and gush, Alex poured from the capsule onto the cave floor, slapping the rock like a dead fish. He did not move.

"Jason! This way. Climb through the hole," Selene yelled, pointing at the opening to her cell. He ran for it, just as Nickelova coiled, stepping over Alex's body as if she didn't even see him in her haste to pursue Jason.

Jason dug his fingers into a crag above the hole and thrust his legs through, but his shoulders caught on the uneven surface. Fuck, what a time to regret gaining the weight back! He reached his arms out, trying his best to collapse his shoulders.

Selene yanked on his hips and jabbed at the stone

around the hole. The dragon eyed him, jaws open. If Jason didn't move, he'd have an upside-down, bent-backward view of his own death. He pushed against the stone, returning the way he'd come, and whirled to face the dragon's teeth.

"Stop, Nickelova," a low voice rasped from the center of the cave. The dragon's head whipped around to face Alex, who glistened in the firelight, his long, dirty-blond curls wet and clinging to his shoulders. "Yeah, it's me."

The dragon roared. Nickelova seemed confused about the reunion. She scratched at the floor and sniffed the air around Alex. He held up his hands and stepped toward her.

"Throw me the amulet, Jason," Alex said. "I'll free you. Nickelova's confused because I'm covered in her magic. She can't smell what I am. But as soon as I'm dry, I'm dragon fodder and so are you."

"Don't trust him," Selene said.

"Be reasonable, Jason. If she kills both of us, she'll simply find another wolf to do her bidding. She's always called the shots. She doesn't need me to bring her plan to fruition, and she doesn't need you. I know how to use the amulet. I can save us both."

"Bullshit. You've never cared for anyone but your-self," Jason snapped.

Alex's eyes drifted to him. "What about you? Do you care about that girl behind you? You may not trust me, but I promise you, the amulet is our only hope of survival, and I'm the only one of the three of us who knows how to use it."

"And you promise to help us?" Jason asked skeptically, eyeing the dragon.

The dragon snorted, a low growl rumbling behind the red and black glint of her scales.

"I promise. For the love of the goddess, our blood is my priority. We are both werewolves. We can work out our differences. Give me a chance to prove to you I've changed."

Alex couldn't be trusted. He was in league with the dragon, likely planning to give her the amulet in exchange for his own life. But as Selene crawled out of her prison behind him, Jason knew he couldn't save her on his own.

And then the dragon stilled, its throat swallowing and its chest glowing red with burgeoning flames. "Jason! I've been locked in a jar for months. I'll never outrun her. If you want to make it out of here alive, you'd best throw me that damned amulet!"

On impulse, Jason removed the amulet from his neck and tossed it to Alex.

"No!" Selene yelled from behind him. "What are you doing?"

TWENTY-SEVEN

Flashing a wicked grin, Alex snatched the amulet from the air and looped it around his neck. The dragon's mouth opened and fire raged toward him. *Pulse.* The flames flowed around Alex as if he were safely locked inside an asbestos bubble.

When the dragon ran out of juice, Alex was left standing among whiffs of steam that curled from the floor. A deep, psychotic laugh echoed through the chamber. "Oh, my dear Nickelova, you have always been full of hot air."

The amulet pulsed again, and Jason stared in disgust as the dragon was skinned alive. In a wave of angry screams, blood, gore, and the break of bones, the reptile was transformed back into a woman. Nickelova lay helpless and naked at his feet, weeping in pain.

"You thought you could replace *me*." Alex spat in her face. "You are nothing compared to me. A fairy with a few magic tricks." His foot connected with her ribs.

"You were weak. I thought you might die. I needed help to continue our plan," she whimpered.

He snorted. "Our. Plan. Key words, Nickelova. Do you know I could see and hear everything in that pickle jar you locked me inside? Don't lie to me. You wanted Jason from the start. Enjoyed his company a little too much when you were doing my dirty work at Hunt Club." He gripped a fistful of her hair and pulled her head off the ground only to slam it back into the floor.

"If you're going to kill her, do it," Jason yelled. He couldn't stand to watch him beat her, no matter what she'd done.

Nickelova sneered. "He's more of a man than you'll ever be."

Alex shook his head. "Ever since we were kids, all the ladies loved Jason. And who are you, sweetheart?" he said to Selene. "Flavor of the month?"

"Don't talk to her." Jason glared at him. "Don't even look at her."

"I'm a fair man," Alex said, his steely eyes flashing in the firelight like a madman's. "A man of my word. I told you I'd help you slay the dragon in exchange for the amulet, and here I am making good. Just one more thing to do." The amulet pulsed, and Alex plunged his hand straight into Nickelova's chest.

For the rest of his life, Jason would remember the scream. Nickelova's mouth opened and a high-pitched shriek erupted from her lips with an edge that seemed to slice right through him.

"By the goddess," Selene murmured. Out of the

corner of his eye, he saw her turn away, unable to watch the horror happening before them.

Alex squeezed and pulled, the tear of flesh and crack of bone making Jason feel almost as ill as the painful gurgle that came from Nickelova's parted lips. The svelte blonde turned her face toward Jason and held out one hand in a plea for help.

"Please," she begged. But there was nothing Jason could do even if he'd wanted to help the woman who'd threatened his pack, his love, and his life.

Alex tore Nickelova's heart from her chest, sending her toppling to the floor, writhing in pain. As he raised the heart above his head, blood ran in rivulets down his arm. The still-beating heart glowed from within like its flesh was wrapped around a gigantic red ruby.

The wound in Nickelova's chest would have been fatal in any other creature, but not in a dragon fae. Freakishly, it filled itself in, her flesh knitting together. The bleeding stopped. The wound transformed from bright red to pale pink. Whimpering, she crawled away from Alex, curling into a ball against the far wall.

Alex's eyes fell on Jason and Selene. "I could kill you. With the smallest effort, I could shatter you like glass. But I'm a man of my word." He gestured toward Nickelova. "The fairy is mortal now. Kill her or leave her to die, I don't care. I don't need her anymore. But this makes us even. And next time I see you, Jason, all bets are off."

Alex headed for the mouth of the cave. Jason followed at a distance until both of them were staring out through the blowing snow. "It's almost nightfall," Alex said into the wind, not bothering to turn and look at Jason. "I wouldn't dally if I were you. If your wolf runs straight down the mountain, he might make the portal before it closes. Her mountain is in Siberia. The only reason you're here is because her magic transported you here. And I'm about to leave with her magic."

"You need to give us time to get out," Jason said. "I don't know the way. I'm not sure my wolf will know how to reach the portal."

Alex flashed a patronizing smile over his shoulder. "Sounds like you have a problem." The amulet pulsed, and he was gone.

Jason ran back into the main chamber and took Selene's hand. "We've got to go. The portal is closing."

"You'll never make it," Nickelova rasped, laughing in a way that seemed painful. "If you leave now, you'll freeze to death before you reach it, and if you wait until you shift, you'll never make it before it closes."

Jason and Selene glanced toward each other and then at the slight, curled form leaning against the wall. Jason strode to her side and held out his hand. "Help us get out of here and I'll see you come to no harm."

Nickelova smiled sadly. "You are such a fucking hero, you know that?" She said the word *hero* like it was a curse. "I am not leaving this cave. And neither are you."

He grabbed her throat.

"Go ahead. Squeeze. What's one more death on your already tarnished soul?" She chuckled.

Selene's hand landed on his arm. "She's not worth it."

His grip tightened. He needed to kill her; it was too dangerous to leave her alive. But he couldn't do it in front of Selene, not with her looking at him like that. He released Nickelova's neck and thought fast. Taking Selene's hand, he ran toward the passageway and navigated to the bedroom where Nickelova had taken him before. "There must be a closet. She must have had gear for Alex even if she had none for herself."

"Here!" Selene rummaged behind the folding screen. There was an entire set of brand-new men's gear. Jason started dressing. Selene dug out yoga pants and a sweater that bagged on her less curvy figure, then donned a pair of snow pants. Jason handed her a puffy white parka.

"The zipper's broken," Selene said.

"I don't imagine she had cause to use it often."

"It's good enough." She shrugged into it. Hat, gloves, and boots later, they made their way toward the cave exit.

"You're not going to like this, but I need to kill her," Jason said. "Alex can control her now that he has her heart. It's not safe leaving her alive."

Selene nodded. "Do what you have to do. I can't watch."

"Understood." Jason balked as they turned the corner into the main chamber. Nickelova was gone. A giant, human-sized cocoon lay where they'd left her. "What the fuck is that?"

"Dear goddess"—Selene's eyes went wide—"she's mummifying herself."

Through a silvery membrane, Jason could see Nick-elova clinging to the dragon scale he'd plucked from her chest with his bone weapon. The same material the amulet was made from. Her eyes were closed, and silver plates were shingling themselves over her from the feet up. Why hadn't he killed her when he had the chance?

Selene removed her glove and knocked her knuckles against the shell forming around the woman. The ring of hollow metal filled the chamber. She glanced toward Jason. "What do we do?"

"We leave her and try to make it to the portal. Come on. We don't have much time."

As the sun sank in the arctic-blue sky, Selene followed Jason out of the mouth of the cave and into the burgeoning storm. They worked their way down the first drop, Jason helping her when her smaller body couldn't reach between handholds and footholds. The climb was nearly vertical, and she struggled to find her grip on the mountain in her boots and gloves. Struggled, until after thirty minutes of grueling effort, her grip failed. At the same time as she heard Jason call out, she dropped, skimming the icy stone and bumping down the side of the mountain.

"Ow! Ahhh!" Her insulated pants ripped, and her shoulder smacked against a sharp crag. Sticky, warm blood oozed from the wound, but the ride didn't stop. Not until she slapped the side of the mountain where the slope leveled off with a back-cracking thump.

"Selene. Selene, are you all right?"

She could hardly hear Jason through the blowing wind. It was a painfully long time before he reached her, and in those minutes, she concentrated on her breathing. In and out. The pain eventually numbed with the cold.

Finally he was at her side. The snow stung her cheeks, but it was her shoulder that worried her. It throbbed. She couldn't move her arm.

"You're bleeding," Jason said.

"I hit my shoulder." She tried to sit up, and a wave of pain and nausea forced her back down. "There's something wrong. I can't move it."

He took a closer look. When he rotated her wrist and tested her range of movement, she cried out. His face paled, and she knew it wasn't because of the dropping temperature. "I'm not a doctor, but it looks dislocated to me."

"Or broken." She frowned toward the setting sun. "No time. Leave me. Find the portal."

"No," he said firmly.

"It's sundown. You can come back for me tomorrow."

"You'll be frozen to death by tomorrow."

"The shift will protect me. My wolf will be fine in this weather."

"And possibly lead you somewhere it's unsafe to shift back. If she can walk at all."

"Come on, Jason," she yelled, tears streaming now.

"Don't fight me on this! We'll never make it out together. For once, just do the smart thing and go! I'm giving you permission to take the easy road."

He laughed and shook his head. "You spoiled me for that, Selene. I never want to do what's easy again. Only what's right. Only what you would do."

She leaned her head back against the rock, cursing.

"I'm going to try to push your arm back into your shoulder socket."

"Do you know how to do that?"

"No, but I've seen it done before. How hard could it be?"

She looked at him worriedly. "Maybe you don't have to. Maybe it will correct itself when I shift."

"Maybe." Jason frowned. "But if it doesn't, I won't be able to correct it in wolf form."

"And if I can't move as a wolf, I'm dead."

"We're dead."

"Your wolf won't necessarily stay. It'll survive, any way it can."

Selene glanced at the mercilessly setting sun.

"It's going to work," Jason said resolutely. Gently he worked her coat off her injured arm. She was still bleeding due to a nasty gash on the back of her shoulder. Hopefully that would heal when she shifted. And if Jason could knock the joint back into place, there was a shred of hope they'd make it out of there alive. He felt down her arm to the joint. Selene tried not to scream, but the pain was nauseating.

"Just do it, Jason!" She could already feel the shift starting, a bubbling grind under her skin.

"I'm sorry about this." He positioned her arm again and gave a fast, hard thrust. This time Selene screamed, a scream that turned into a howl. The shift was coming. Her shoulder felt oddly warm, although her arm still wasn't working properly.

"Is it any better?" Jason pitched forward, the shift turning his green eyes to amber. He unzipped his jacket in the throes of transformation.

She used her good hand to strip out of the winter clothes, following his lead. "I still can't move it, but it doesn't hurt as much." Bent in half, her jaw elongated as the snow stung her naked flesh.

"I love you, Selene." Jason's claws sprouting from his knuckles. His distorted hands landed in the snow.

"I didn't fully believe you when you said it before," she said, the need to confess gripping her heart. "I thought I was just another passing fancy, temporary entertainment for your vice."

"That's not true."

"When you left with Nickelova tonight, I thought you were joining up with her. I thought you couldn't resist her."

He shook his head. "I had to—" He groaned as tawny fur broke out across his inner arms.

"I said yes before on Rivergate grounds because I wanted you so badly I was willing to lose everything, even if I might have you for only a short time," she rambled.

She had to tell him, had to get it out. "I never thought I could want someone again. I thought I was ruined for love after what happened to me... the things I did. But I believe you now. I love you too, Jason. Forever." White fur climbed her arms, over her shoulders, between her breasts.

If Jason said anything else, she didn't hear it. Her last thoughts were that she wasn't cold anymore. And then the wolf took over and she wasn't Selene anymore.

TWENTY-EIGHT

The white wolf's consciousness was part instinct, part chemistry, and part body language. With a soul of total freedom, she sped down the mountain, ignoring the slight ache in her shoulder that gave her a pronounced limp. The dark wolf, her mate, was by her side, smelling of thick fur and hunger. Yes, hunger. It was time to hunt.

She whimpered and the dark wolf with the tawny belly licked her face before scanning the mountain for movement; a rabbit or bird would be a fine meal. Her leathery nose opened and sniffed the air. There was something on the wind. Exotic. Close. The dark wolf must have smelled it too because his head snapped around.

The source of the smell came from a bird, a huge bird that flapped its gigantic black wings in the blowing snow. The wolves stalked forward, hunting the black thing that folded and snapped in the wind. All at once the black wings expanded, then settled like a heavy fog around the form of a woman. The white wolf stopped. This was not food. This was danger and power. With jet-black hair and a dress that seemed to hold itself up by magic alone, the woman pinned the wolves with her icy blue stare.

"My good and faithful daughter," she said, approaching. "Do not be afraid." The white wolf bowed to the woman, a deep instinct driving her to revere what she didn't fully understand. The woman's hand came to rest on the wolf's head. "You must follow me now. This place is no longer safe for you."

The dark-haired woman turned and strode down the mountain, the wolves heeling at her side. Miles passed. The white wolf's stomach growled, but she did not stray from the one who led her away. The darker wolf whimpered. His whine made her nervous, but the pull the mysterious woman had over both of them trumped her bond with him. They followed with an instinctual trust.

And then a ripple cut through the night, constricting like a closing mouth of darkness.

"Come, daughter. Bring your love. I will hold it open for you." The woman pulled back the corner of the night sky and motioned for the wolves to pass through. The dark wolf leaped through first, disappearing somewhere into the beyond. The white wolf stepped forward and licked the woman's hand.

"You are welcome, dear one. Now you must go. You've done me a service. Go reap your reward."

The wolf raised her paws to jump through but

paused when a man appeared across from the woman, a man with thick, twisting horns that grew from the sides of his head.

"Meddling again in the fate of this world, Hecate? I might think you weren't taking our agreement seriously," the horned man said. He was hulking and horrifying. His mere presence made the white wolf shiver.

The woman's gaze shifted to the white wolf. "Go. Now!"

The wolf leaped through the portal, feet leaving snow but landing on bright green grass. When she turned around, the woman's fingers retracted from the tear in the darkness. The white wolf stared at the place she'd just entered through. She needed to remember something, something important. But a moment later, the portal was gone.

A moment after that, the memory of the portal grew distant and faded entirely. All there was in the world was the dark wolf, her mate, who jogged to her side with a bloody rabbit between his teeth.

Bright, warm light pierced Jason's closed eyelids, but he fought the urge to wake up. He was happy. Worn out, muscles sore, he relished the after-shift euphoria, his body flooded with endorphins counteracting the last shift of the month. He stretched hard and lean in the soft grass, rolling onto his side.

And then, with a start, he remembered. The mountain, the storm, Selene. He opened his eyes and frantically searched for her. But he needn't look far. She was right beside him, curled into his side as if she still had a tail. He stroked the short strands of her hair back from her face and ran his hands down her naked body, searching for injuries. The gash on the back of her shoulder was already a pink scar. Everything else looked okay.

"I like this way of saying good morning," she whispered, rolling into his embrace.

"We made it. Oh, thank the goddess, we made it." Jason exhaled. "How's your shoulder?"

"It's fine. You fixed me. And I think the goddess is exactly who we have to thank."

"Hmm?" Jason was distracted by the way her body shifted under his as if it was something she'd done every day of her waking life. She rolled him on top of her and wrapped her legs around his hips. He balanced on his elbows so that he wouldn't crush her.

"I have a memory, a wolf memory. It's a slippery thing, like a forgotten dream, but I seem to remember the goddess, Hecate, showing us the way out. Do you remember that?"

Jason shook his head. "No. But I think I remember catching a rabbit."

She laughed beneath him, and the jiggle of her body did all sorts of things to his libido. His erection kicked against her lower belly. "Selene... I love you."

"I love you too." She looked into his eyes. They were nose to nose and chest to chest, but it was the connection between them that made it the most intimate position he'd ever been in with a woman.

"You once told me that the only way to conquer a vice is to discover the need it's trying to fill and fill it with something else."

She nodded. "An anchor, a feeling or experience that fills you with light and keeps you from the darkness. We found yours. The memory of your family when you were all together."

"The thing is..." He stroked her hair back, taking his time to choose his words carefully. "I don't think that memory is strong enough to anchor me anymore."

"No?"

"No. That memory is marred with darkness, with loss, with regret," he said. "But I have one that is strong enough. A new memory."

He met her gaze, that violet blue as intense as he'd ever seen it. "When I was in that room with Nickelova, there was a moment when I felt my vice fighting for control. I needed an anchor, and when I closed my eyes, all I saw was you. You're my true mate, Selene. I felt the bond the first time I saw you, and I feel it even stronger now. You're my true north, the light to my soul, bright enough to stave off the darkness, pure enough to be the only anchor I'll ever need."

"Oh, Jason. I feel it too. But... it's okay if you hold the memory of your parents above me. It's not a competition. They loved you first," she said seriously.

"Yes. Yes. I'll never forget them or that perfect day you reminded me of. But an anchor, an anchor should be powerful enough to root your soul. You are that thing for me now. I may be able to exist without you, but I can't live, not really." He licked his lips, trying to convey to her exactly what he was feeling. "They loved me first, but I want you to love me last and always."

"I do. I will." She squinted. "What are you saying?"

"I don't just want you to move out of Sanctuary. I want you to move in with me. I want to wine you and dine you and fly you around the world and dance with you in my kitchen every night. I want to give you all the experiences you never had growing up. And in time, when you are sick of dating me, I want to marry you."

Selene's mouth dropped open, a confused smile flashing briefly. "You do?"

"Say yes, Selene. Say you'll be mine and only mine, for always."

Her mouth worked, but no sound came out. Jason started to wonder if her answer was no. He pulled back slightly, unsure if he should remove his hand from where it rested on her ribs.

"Yes. Yes, Jason," she blurted, catching his wrist and holding his hand in place. "I'll be your anchor. I'll be your anchor because you've become mine." She grabbed his face and pulled it to hers, her lips parting to let his kiss in.

Jason wanted their first time to be special. Dinner, flowers, candlelight, hours of worshipping every inch of her creamy flesh. Not in the forest after a near-death experience. But Selene had other plans. He thought she'd be hesitant, maybe scared, considering her history. He was wrong. She grabbed his hips and demanded his full and undivided attention.

"Are you... sure...?" he stuttered, then gave in to her insistent pull on his body. "Oh. Game on."

His breath hitched as he entered her, her tight heat making him work for it. Inch by glorious inch he eased into her, until finally, after what seemed like a small eternity, he was fully seated inside her. Finally complete.

He'd been with women before, hundreds of women actually, but as he connected with her, he realized he'd been deceived. All the sex he'd had in the past had been plastic imitations of the real thing. The intimate connection he held in his arms blew every other experience away.

Working his arm under the small of her back, he lifted her, supporting her beneath him as he worked a better angle. She hooked her ankles behind him and wrapped her arms around his neck, clinging to him. The scent of mango and vanilla wafted from her skin. He buried his face in what remained of her hair.

She thrust up against him. "Harder. I won't break."

He lifted her, guiding her until he was balanced on his knees with her straddling his hips. Deeper this way, he held nothing back, reveling in the tiny moans she produced with each targeted thrust. Selene's violet eyes sparked with passion as she came crashing down on him in a wave of flawless skin and delicate bones. He moved inside her, allowing her to wash over him, to draw him higher, to the peak, to the place he was tempted to tumble over.

"Oh no, not yet," she said, slowing her movements. "I've waited too long for you to rush this. I want more."

"I want all of you Selene. Again and again. I want to feel that you're mine."

He held himself back, circling his hips to keep from going over the edge. Cupping her under the thighs, he lifted, standing from the soft grass and supporting her against his chest. The trunk of the tree they'd woken under made a fine brace for one foot, his hand resting on the trunk. In this position, he was so deep inside her he feared he'd hurt her. But she only gripped him tighter. When she scored his back with her nails, he didn't hold back.

She moaned in his ear, pulling on his shoulders to ride the rhythm. He lost himself in her, in the connection that was everything he always wanted and never knew he was missing.

SELENE MET JASON THRUST FOR THRUST, HER ARMS STRAINING to draw him closer, her abs working to build the momentum, her mouth melding with his until she'd explored every inch of his mouth and neck. And still she wanted more.

She'd never known it could be like this, to be completely filled both emotionally and physically. Her body could not contain the love he poured into her. She was a bowl overflowing with light, a light that shone in all her dark corners, smoothed her jagged edges, and made her feel like all the pain of the past served a purpose—to bring her to this point of total ecstasy.

A new urgency quickened his thrusts, and she found his eyes had bled amber and his expression had become markedly possessive. The look alone sent her over the edge.

"You're *mine*, Selene." His possessive growl rattled her bones, and then he bit down on the place her shoulder met her neck, marking her, claiming her. The bond snapped into place, no longer a simple magnetic pull but a chain, linking them, binding them. She leaned her head back and came apart, shattering in his arms with his teeth still in her flesh, his hot skin against hers, his arms the only thing holding her up.

She felt his orgasm like a rush within her, and the effect was intense. Her body clenched around him, spilling over with pleasure once more. She clung to him through the aftershocks, where she ended and he began becoming a blur in her mind.

After a long time, she slid off his body and onto her own feet. "By the goddess," she whispered.

Jason rested his forehead against hers. "By the goddess, indeed."

They were still recovering when a sound came on the wind.

"Jason!" A man's voice called from a distance. Selene looked around the tree in the direction of the noise. Silas, Laina, and Gerty were headed toward them.

"Hmm." He smiled down at her. "Looks like we've been rescued."

TWENTY-NINE

"He has her heart?" Laina cried once they'd filled both her and Silas in on what had happened.

Jason placed a finger over his lips when the patrons of the coffee shop where they'd chosen to meet turned to stare at their table. Dressed and rested, he and Selene had spent the past hour detailing their ordeal, and only now did his siblings seem to grasp the scope of what occurred.

"What were you thinking, Jason? How could you hand over the amulet like that?" Silas kept his voice low, but Jason had no trouble hearing the venom in it.

"He had no choice." The acerbic tone of Selene's voice captured Silas's attention, and Jason preened at his mate's willingness to defend him. "Jason couldn't use the amulet. It takes some kind of additional magic to operate. We were naked, trapped in a dragon's lair on the side of a mountain in Siberia without any means of defense. If Jason had let Nickelova fry Alex, we would have been next."

"And believe me," Jason said, "I thought about falling on my sword for the pack. But once Nickie killed us, she'd have the amulet back. It was only a matter of time before she'd find another werewolf to take Alex's place."

"But she's dead, right?" Laina asked.

Jason ran a hand over his face. "No. Not exactly."

Selene wrapped her fingers around his forearm and squeezed. "Nickelova didn't die when Alex removed her heart; she became mortal. We could have killed her... but we thought we needed her to get back through the portal. By the time we realized what she was doing, it was too late."

Silas rubbed his temples and sighed deeply. "So she's mortal but she survived?"

"During the fight," Jason explained, "I dislodged a scale from her dragon form. She used it to form some kind of cocoon around herself."

Silas growled. "So not only is Alex still at large, but Nickelova is a ticking time bomb in a mountain somewhere."

"How much do you want to bet that Alex returns her heart to her at some point and wakes her up? I imagine a girl will do a lot for a heart," Laina said.

"I'm sorry to have to share this, but..." Jason glanced at Selene. "It makes her his slave. If he does rescue her and she comes out of that... thing she's in, she'll be forced to obey him."

Silas cursed.

Selene squeezed his hand in support, narrowing a hard stare on his brother and sister. The look she gave Silas alone could solder iron. "I don't have any family. But if I did, I think I'd be a lot happier to have them home safely." Selene shifted her gaze, pointing a finger at Laina's nose. "Your brother almost died last night."

Silas sighed. "We're happy to have you back. Both of you. But this changes everything. As alpha, I'm just a little nervous about what this means for the pack. We may need to go into hiding again."

"No," Laina said. "Not again." Tears pooled in her eyes. "Kyle and I have just started to make a life for ourselves. He finally has new clients for his treehouse business. I can't ask him to trash everything he's worked for, and I certainly can't close Four Paws again."

"I'll talk to Grateful and see if there's anything we can do to strengthen the wards around Rivergate," Silas said. "I'm disappointed Nickelova could see and hear these two from beyond the boundary. We've got to protect ourselves."

"I'll talk to Gerty," Laina said. "If Nickelova leveraged the curse she had on Jason to find him, maybe Gerty knows how to make sure Alex can't use that in the future now that he has her heart."

There was a long silence. Jason stared into his coffee, tapping out a song on the side of his cup. Part of him agreed with Silas that he'd put the pack in danger when he pursued Nickelova on his own. But as he glanced at Selene, the steam from her coffee curling along the fine bones of her jaw, all he could think was he'd do it again.

Silas cleared his throat and stared pointedly at Jason and Selene's coupled hands. "Not to be the chaperone at the dance who taste tests the punch, but it seems like there's another topic of conversation that needs to be broached. What's going on with you two?"

"I'LL BE FOREVER GRATEFUL FOR WHAT YOU DID FOR ME, Artemis," Selene said as she packed up her room into the same brown plaid bag she'd used since childhood. "I'm sorry if I was a disappointment."

"A disappointment? You?" Artemis raised her eyebrows. "Never. *I* could never be disappointed in you. But do you know who you have disappointed?"

"Who?"

"All the Fireborn families with girls Jason's age. They've had to say goodbye to the dream that their daughters might one day snare a spot as the next princess. He's taken. Permanently."

Selene sighed. "I didn't set out with a goal of loving Jason. It just happened. It crept up on me like some wonderful dream as if one moment I was drifting to sleep and the next I was in his arms."

"What causes people to fall in love? Is it chemistry? Opportunity? The hand of the goddess herself?" Artemis wrapped an arm around her shoulders and squeezed. "All we know for sure is that love is precious and should not be denied. You found your mate. Your true, fated mate. That's a gift from the goddess herself."

"It's frightening though. I'm leaving the only life I've ever really known and loved behind to go shack up with a guy who just recently recovered from a major vice. It sounds crazy when I say it out loud."

The older woman smiled. "One must be brave to truly love. What you set out to do is not easy work. It's not magic. Loving someone is seeing them for who they truly are, the light and the dark, and inviting all of it, the whole person, into your life unconditionally. You can leave or protect yourself if things go wrong, Selene, but true love will stay with you. It will be a beacon that leads you back to him again and again. You'll always demand the best of him, always pick him up when he falls, always ask the goddess to protect him, and he'll do the same for you if he truly loves you."

Selene nodded, a memory blowing into her thoughts like a cool breeze. "Speaking of the goddess, I had a strange experience I need to ask you about."

Artemis folded into a chair at the small table in her dormitory. Selene sat across from her and rested her coupled hands on the table. "What is it?"

"When Jason and I were escaping from Nickelova's lair, I was in wolf form, but I swear I remember seeing the goddess lead us to safety."

"What did she look like?"

"Tall, curvy, with long waves of wild black hair and a dress that clung like a black fog around her, as if it was cut from the night itself. The wind had no effect on her—it didn't even rustle her hair. And although Jason and I had almost frozen to death before the shift, she didn't seem cold at all. She called me her dear one."

"That certainly sounds like the goddess."

"She led us to the portal, but before I could pass through, I noticed a man standing across from her."

Artemis stiffened. "What sort of man?"

"A man with large twisting horns growing from his head, like a ram but different, straighter. He was naked from the waist up. Hairy. And his eyes were black and dull as coal. He told her she was interfering and that was against their agreement."

Artemis stood and paced the small room.

"I don't usually remember things from my wolf form. I'm wondering if my brain simply produced this to fill in the gaps of an emotionally trying night. It couldn't possibly have been real, could it?."

"Oh, I fear what you saw was quite real. In fact, I'm sure of it."

"How?"

Artemis frowned. "We don't teach about the horned god here, but there's no way you could describe him as perfectly as you have without seeing him firsthand."

"The horned god?"

"He goes by many names, but in our tradition, he is called Panaal." Artemis spread her hands. "All existence must maintain balance."

"Of course. The goddess demands balance in all things."

"Not just the goddess. Everything. From the largest beast to the tiniest cell, balance is the most fundamental of laws. Disrupt the balance and things start to deteriorate. Everything, all the interdependencies of life begin to change, to adapt until a new balance is found. Panaal is the balance to Hecate, the masculine to her feminine, the keeper of the underworld."

Selene's shoulders drooped. "I don't understand. I thought Hecate was her own balance. The maiden, the mother, and the crone. Protector of women. Goddess of the crossroads. Mother to all supernatural beings."

"If Hecate is all about balance and order, Panaal is all about the wild, about chaos, about all creatures' primal needs. He is the source of the raw instincts that drive us all in the absence of intelligence and civilization. He is the hunter where our goddess is the healer. He thrives on disorder. He desires turmoil. He loves war."

"Sounds like a real ball of fun," Selene said, swallowing. "What do you think it means that he was in my memory?"

"I'm not sure, but I don't think it's a coincidence that he arrived after Alex took Nickelova's heart. Panaal sees opportunity. The balance is shifting. A werewolf has a fairy heart, and the goddess has helped you escape almost certain death."

"Is it just me, or does this situation make your spine tingle?" Selene asked.

Artemis shivered. "I fear that heart has far greater value than the amulet Alex had before and far greater consequences for our pack."

THIRTY

Outside Sanctuary, Selene smiled when she saw Jason waiting for her, parked in the sleek sports car she thought looked like a drivable piece of art. He rolled down the passenger's side window as she approached and sneered at her brown plaid bag.

"Are you sure you want to bring that thing? I thought I'd take you shopping today to replace everything inside it."

"Everything?"

"Everything you'll let me... with the exception of that navy-blue number you wore when you made me cookies. We'll keep it for sentimental reasons."

"I think I'll keep all of it," she said through a smug smile. "For sentimental reasons."

He climbed out and lifted the bag from her hands, snorting when all her worldly possessions fit easily in the Bugatti's meager trunk space. He hurried to open the door for her, then climbed behind the wheel.

"I have one quick stop to see a client before lunch. Are you game for Valentine's restaurant?"

"I've never been," she said truthfully.

He straightened in the leather seat like the idea was sacrilege. "Oh, Selene, we must rectify this situation. Chef Logan Valentine makes a chocolate cake that will positively light your fire." His eyes raked down the torso of her plain gray dress.

With one raised eyebrow, she stroked down her leg and allowed her fingers to tug her hem up to midthigh. "Too late."

Jason's smile faded to a darker expression as his gaze caressed her thigh. But he didn't touch her. Instead, he started the engine and drove away, merging onto the road that led into the city. Had he lost interest in her already? Her gaze drifted out the window as the car sped forward, embarrassment warming her cheeks. What was she thinking? This wasn't the time or the place.

But then his hand was on her inner thigh, his palm caressing north, pulling her dress even higher. "I didn't think Artemis would enjoy the show. She was watching you through the upstairs window."

"Oh," she said. The word turned into a moan as his fingers found her center, rubbing over her simple cotton underwear.

"You're wet already. I've barely gotten started."

She moved against his hand, grinding into his fingers until he repositioned to oblige her. What was it about the way he touched her that incinerated all former rationality? She'd gone years without sex and now could think of nothing but Jason and making up for lost time. Selene whimpered and ran a hand between her breasts.

A passing car honked and Jason overcorrected the wheel. "I better pull over before I kill someone. Has anyone ever told you, you're very distracting?"

"Never." She smiled at him and licked her lips. He overcorrected again.

Both hands firmly on the wheel, Jason took the next exit, but Selene wasn't in the mood for waiting. She'd waited long enough for her true mate, for a relationship where she could safely express herself. She didn't plan to wait another minute.

She reached over and unzipped his fly, freeing his erection and sliding her fingers along his shaft.

"Selene," he murmured.

She leaned over, ducking her head beneath his elbow and taking his cock into her mouth. She'd never done this before in a car. Never done anything like this before on purpose, driven by her own desires. She relished it, sucking and licking—the power she had over him—as he began to moan her name in earnest.

The car stopped, but Selene didn't. She hastened the rhythm, feeding off the rush of his breathing and the way he slapped the ceiling of the car. She watched him writhe out of the corner of her eye as she mercilessly drove his cock into the back of her throat.

And then he shattered. She swallowed what he gave her, savoring the command she had of his body. He was hers. Putty in her hands. Her lids sank as the tremors rippled through him and he looked at her like she made the world spin simply by breathing.

"By the goddess, Selene, you are full of surprises."

"Just making up for lost time." She grinned.

She slid back into her own seat. "Holy mother-of-pearl!" Selene almost hit the roof. A figure stood in front of their car in the alley where Jason had parked. The menacing form hovered in the shadow of the building, almost blending into the darkness.

"It's okay. It's Ryker."

"He wasn't watching, was he?"

Jason zipped his pants. "Well, he wasn't there when I parked the car."

Heat flooded Selene's cheeks.

"Believe me, there's nothing to be embarrassed about. This guy has seen worse. Way worse."

She straightened her dress and climbed out of the car. Ryker moved toward them, his forward momentum out of sync with his actual steps as if he were traveling a moving walkway.

"Jason... so glad to see you survived your encounter with your jaded dragon lover." Although Ryker spoke to Jason, his eyes never left Selene. He stared at her, entranced, licking his lips occasionally.

"Er, thanks," Jason said awkwardly.

"Nice to... see you again," Selene said, almost sputtering.

Ryker's dark eyes flashed red. "It is my sincere pleasure." The man brought his full lips to the back of her hand, her skin heating where the kiss connected. She rubbed the area, which itched like it had endured a minor burn. "And, may I say, the shorter style suits you." He gestured toward her hair.

Selene ran a hand through the sleek pixie cut she'd gotten to even out her butchered tresses. She wasn't sure she'd keep it, but it was nice to know someone appreciated the look.

"Have you heard the news? Selene is no longer an acolyte; she's my fiancée." Jason drew her against his side and away from Ryker.

"Fiancée?" He licked his lips. "This *is* a happy turn of events. Come inside," he said. "I assume you've brought me something."

Jason patted the pocket of his suit jacket and nodded.

Ryker turned the corner and entered the shop Selene had visited before. Daylight had done nothing to reduce the creepiness of Lost Things. The antique sign squeaked on its hinges above her head, and she noticed what looked like a new, smaller human skull in the window display.

"What exactly do you sell here, Ryker?" she asked curiously. "I didn't ask you before."

"No. You were too busy threatening my life in exchange for finding your man."

Selene frowned.

"Ah, never mind. The excuse to set foot in Soleil's brothel was payment enough for my services." He lowered his voice. "She doesn't care for me."

"Personality conflict?" Selene asked.

"As an incubus, I feed off sexual energy. The clients

might not notice, but it drains the girls." He smiled wickedly. "Thank you, by the way. For earlier." He gestured in the direction their car was parked. "And they say there's no such thing as a free lunch."

Selene felt her cheeks blaze with the hot sting of a blush.

He approached her, inhaling deeply. When he spoke again, his voice was flinty and his breath carried a hint of sulfur. "To answer your first question, I am a purveyor of antiquities: rare magical objects and forgotten and out-of-print texts on the supernatural. Feel free to examine the merchandise, but don't touch. Some of my inventory can be... temperamental."

She nodded slowly. "Wouldn't dream of it." She focused on a dehydrated monkey's paw.

"Now, Jason." Ryker held out one hand sporting long, tapered fingers with nails filed to a point.

Jason removed a silver cylinder from his pocket and placed it in Ryker's palm.

"What is this?"

"This is the weapon that you lent me. I was unable to use it."

"Our agreement, Jason, was that I would lend you this enchanted weapon in exchange for a fairy's heart. Are you telling me you did not uphold your end of the bargain?"

"I'm saying I wasn't able to use your weapon, and thus, I didn't get the heart. I'm returning the weapon."

"Where is the heart?"

Jason narrowed his eyes. "What makes you believe it's not still beating in Nickelova's chest?"

Selene wouldn't have thought it possible, but Ryker's expression darkened even further. The incubus gave off an aura that was both the darkest red she'd ever encountered and cold as ice. Cold fire. That's how she'd describe him. A wild, icy absence of humanity.

"I can *feel* it." His voice was harsh. "You don't have it with you, but it's close. Very close. Did you hide it from me? Did you think I wouldn't know?"

Jason's eyes widened. "You feel it now? Here?"

"Since early this morning." Ryker rubbed a circle over the left side of his chest. "The air is thick with it, a heady perfume of power that makes my skin tingle."

"Alex Bloodright stole that heart," Jason said. "Do you think you can lead us to it? He'll be where the heart is."

Ryker examined Jason and then Selene. "You're telling the truth."

"Of course I'm telling the truth. I'd give you the heart if I had it, but Alex took it. If he's here, we need to stop him."

Ryker sniffed the air. He strode out of the store, the door chiming above their heads, and turned slowly on the sidewalk. His tattoo smoldered through the right sleeve of his shirt, the round curves and geometric shapes of an ancient symbol glowing through the posh fabric. "I thought you were hiding the heart from me for your own purposes."

"I never had the heart. Alex cut it out of Nickelova and left us to die. We barely made it out alive."

Ryker assessed Jason, eyes blazing. "Very well. I'll lead you there." Ryker extended his hand. "Alex is yours. But the heart is mine."

"And then we're square?"

Ryker nodded.

"Deal." Jason shook the demon's hand. Selene had a bad feeling about this. Was it a good idea to make a deal with a demon?

Ryker motioned for them to follow as he drifted down the street in that unusually fluid way he moved, turning left down the next alley.

"Are you sure about this?" Selene whispered to Jason. "He's a demon, like from the underworld. How do you know he's not manipulating you?"

"He's not from the underworld. He's from New Jersey," Jason whispered.

"Huh?"

"His mother was human." He glanced in her direction. "I gave him the loan to start Lost Things. We got to know each other."

"Can we trust him? He almost killed you with that snake ring."

Jason took a deep breath and let it out through his nose. "Ryker's help is often complicated. But he's an incredibly useful friend to have."

"By the goddess." Selene lowered her chin and squeezed Jason's hand harder.

"This is the vampire district. Why would Alex come here?" Jason mused.

"It's the middle of the day. Most of the local residents are sleeping," Selene said. "If he came earlier this morning, there's no place safer."

"Or a vampire is helping him," Jason said.

Ryker looked both ways before climbing three stairs to reach the entrance to an apartment complex. He sniffed, then tried the door—locked. Selene perused the intercom system, noting it was labeled with symbols instead of names.

"Don't bother," Ryker said to her. "Everyone who lives here is snug inside their coffin for the day with the exception of the man you're looking for, and I'd rather not call his attention to our presence."

"So how do we get in?" Jason asked.

Ryker's brow puckered, that wicked grin turning his full lips. With a twist of his neck, his entire body transformed into a column of smoke that filtered under the door and re-formed inside. He unlocked and opened the door for them.

"That must come in handy," Selene said.

The demon held a long, tapered finger to his lips. "Shhh."

They followed him up the stairs, Selene rolling her footsteps to keep them as quiet as possible. Jason did the same. Ryker's feet never seemed to fully make contact with the floor.

When they reached apartment 5A, Ryker stopped. He

glanced at Jason and did the disappearing smoke act again. The lock clicked slowly, and the door opened.

Jason motioned to Selene to wait where she was. She shook her head. Not a chance. They drifted into the apartment, but it was completely empty. Not so much as a chair in the main room.

Selene turned to Jason in confusion and caught a streak of blue moving out from behind the door. "Look out!"

Alex's joined hands pounded the back of Jason's skull, sending him toppling forward. Instead of falling flat on his stomach, he tucked and rolled. Selene shuffled out of the way as Ryker blew through Alex like a dark wind and disappeared. So much for a show of solidarity. While Alex shook off the sting of sulfur, Selene went for the amulet. She planted her bare foot on his stomach, snatched the dragon scale, and lifted. It slid over his head easily enough, but his hand shot out and caught the chain.

"Not yours, wolf bitch." Alex sneered at her before wrapping his hand in the chain and yanking, hard. Her slight weight tumbled into the wall.

Jason jumped onto Alex's back, his bigger size dwarfing the rogue wolf's sickly physique. One, two quick punches to the werewolf's temple and Jason had him by the throat. Alex spun away and stumbled backward toward the window, holding his neck with one hand and his side with the other.

"Still hurting, Alex?" Jason asked, approaching slowly. "Maybe you needed another month in Nickelova's pickle jar. I don't have one of those for you to heal in, but the pack has a nice strong prison cell."

Alex donned the amulet again. "I could kill you, blow you apart. But we worked together to fight Nickelova, Jason. We'd be stronger if we joined forces now. I don't want to hurt you."

Selene focused in on a bead of sweat at Alex's temple. It rolled down the side of his face, followed by another. His muscles twitched like he could barely hold himself up.

"You *can't* hurt us," Selene said. "Not without hurting yourself even more."

Alex took a step back.

"All magic comes with a price. Using that amulet costs you, and judging by your appearance, you've paid a high one the past couple of days. You're even more emaciated than you were only days ago. You might be able to use magic against us, but the process could kill you."

Jason took another step forward. "Where's the heart?"

Baring his teeth, Alex said, "Somewhere safe."

A black mist collected between them. Ryker. He held up a still throbbing mass of red flesh Selene knew was Nickelova's heart. "Mm-hmm. Yes. It was in a safe, hidden under the floorboards in the bedroom." The incubus grinned. "Finders keepers." He glanced between Alex and Jason, his barbed tail sweeping the air behind him.

"No!" Alex cried and dove for the heart. Ryker gave

him a patronizing wave before dissolving from within his arms, heart and all.

Jason used the distraction to his advantage. He plowed his shoulder into Alex with a righteous howl. They scuffled toward the window where Alex gripped Jason by the shoulders and yanked.

"Watch out!" Selene screamed, but it was too late. Glass shattered and the two wolves tumbled through the fifth-story window.

Selene ran to the edge, searching the sidewalk below. Alex was gone, and Jason lay face down on the concrete. "Jason!"

THIRTY-ONE

Selene thundered down the steps loud enough to wake the dead. Only, in this neighborhood, it was the undead she had to worry about. Luckily, if any of the vampires inside the apartments she passed did wake, they didn't bother emerging from their afternoon's rest. She raced to Jason's side, just as he was pushing himself up off the concrete.

"Are you hurt? Maybe you shouldn't move." Glancing up at the hole that was the fifth-floor window, she examined his body, searching for signs of injury.

"I'm okay." Jason brushed himself off. "Alex used the amulet to break his fall before he blinked out of here. I only fell a couple of feet. It didn't feel good, but I'm not damaged."

"Thank the goddess." Selene pressed a hand to her chest.

"Silas isn't going to be happy to learn Alex got away again." Jason ran a hand through his hair in frustration.

"Silas needs to count his blessings. By the look of Alex's aura, he's going to be underground for a while. The man was sick. Very, very sick."

"Yeah?"

"His entire being was surrounded by a dirty gray halo. He wasn't completely healed. My guess is that he'll be searching for a healer to finish what Nickelova started. He's not strong enough to go far. Silas will find him. Plus, thanks to you, Alex no longer has Nickelova's heart."

Jason's face fell. "Speaking of the heart..." He took her hand, pulling her in the direction of Lost Things. He called Ryker's name as soon as he walked through the door.

"Back so soon?" The demon appeared between two piles of antique crap, looking quite pleased with himself.

"No thanks to you."

"What part of our agreement led you to believe I'd help you kill Alex?"

Jason shook his head. "The heart..."

"Is mine. That was our agreement."

"What do you plan to do with it?"

Ryker gave a knowing smile. "Save it for a rainy day. A treasure like that could be dangerous in the wrong hands. I intend to keep it in the right ones. Mine." He flourished his fingers in the air.

Jason nodded. "I trust you'll let me know if anything changes in that department. No matter what Alex or anyone else offers you, give me a chance to top it before you let it go."

Ryker looked confused for a moment, then answered in a slow and steady tone. "The heart is not for sale, Mr. Flynn. I plan to keep it for my own purposes. But I want you to know, I cherish our relationship and won't let it fall into the wrong hands. You can count on me to keep it safe. Now can I interest you in a gift for your lovely new mate? Perhaps a candle that tells your future in its smoke?" He lifted a black wax taper from a pile beside him.

"No," Selene said firmly, pulling Jason toward the door. "Thank you, Ryker, but we have to go."

"Very well. A pleasure to see you again, Selene. Good luck with your new... situation."

The door chimed as it closed behind them and they headed, hand in hand, back to the car.

Two weeks later...

"One more bite?" Jason held a forkful of Valentine's chocolate cake in front of Selene's lips, his hand cupped beneath her chin to keep any crumbs from falling onto the sheets. After an afternoon of shopping, they'd stopped at their now-favorite restaurant, Valentine's, for dinner to go.

"Ugh, it's delicious, but I can't. I'm so full."

It had been two weeks since he'd tackled Alex through the window—two weeks since they'd moved in together—and Jason couldn't remember ever being happier.

"I love to watch you eat."

"Really?" She laughed.

"Really. The thought of providing for you is oddly satisfying." He leaned over her, stroking the delicate space between her eye and her cheekbone with the back of his fingers. "I want to give you the best of everything until the shine coming off of you tells everyone you're mine."

Selene glanced around the room at the dozens of packages lined up against the wall of their bedroom. "The things you buy me won't say I'm yours." She laughed when his face fell in horror. "But I will. I'll tell everyone."

He kissed her softly. "I like that. I plan to do the same. Speaking of telling people, I was thinking we could get married next summer, in Italy. We can go there first. Soon. Find the perfect place."

"Italy? But... I need to find a job. I'm not an acolyte anymore. I thought you could help me choose a new career."

He lifted his eyebrows. "You don't have to work. Not unless you want to."

"I want to! I have to have something to do while you're doing what you do."

His face turned serious, and he gave her a long, hard look. "What is it that you're passionate about?" In all his years as an investor, he'd learned the most successful careers and companies were based on passion. He wouldn't let her settle for anything less.

She stared at the ceiling for a moment. "Other than studying the goddess, I'd have to say baking. I love to bake."

Jason gave her an ear-to-ear grin. "Perfect. My company will fund your bakery start-up. Step one: research other bakeries. I recommend we start in Italy, perhaps with a side trip to a culinary school in France."

She giggled. "Italy. What a coincidence." She shrugged. "Fine. I guess I have to start somewhere."

"Me too." He kissed her neck in earnest.

"Haven't you had enough?" Selene joked as his lips worked their way down her body once more.

He stopped and locked eyes with her, allowing all levity to bleed from his expression. For weeks he'd analyzed his wolf, waiting for his vice to return with a vengeance. Waiting to want another woman so badly that he'd have to lock himself in his bedroom again to stop from hurting Selene. But that day hadn't come. All he wanted, all his wolf wanted, was her.

"Yes and no," he said. She quirked an eyebrow. "Yes, *you* are enough for me. Just you. Forever."

She smiled sheepishly. "And no?"

"No, I have not had enough... of you."

She squealed with joy as he pulled her beneath him once more, her body quickly melding with his. Threading his fingers into hers above her head, he dedicated himself to making her believe she was the only woman in his universe.

• • •

Thank you for reading **FERAL INSTINCTS**. Alex is still out there and Silas has never been under more pressure to protect his pack. Read a bonus epilogue featuring Silas here:

And preorder Silas's story FOREVER MATED here.

FOREVER MATED
THE WOLVES OF FIREBORN PACK
USA TODAY BESTSELLING AUTHOR
GENEVIEVE JACK

MEET GENEVIEVE JACK

USA Today bestselling and multi-award winning author Genevieve Jack writes wild, witty, and wicked-hot paranormal romance and romantic fantasy. She believes there's magic in every breath we take and probably something supernatural living in most dark basements. You can summon her with coffee, wine, and books, but she sticks around for dogs and chocolate. Her novels feature badass heroines, fiercely loyal heroes, and fantasy elements that will fill you with wonder. Learn more at GenevieveJack.com.

Do you know Jack? Keep in touch to stay in the know about new releases, sales, and giveaways.

facebook.com/AuthorGenevieveJack

instagram.com/authorgenevievejack

bookbub.com/authors/genevieve-jack

tiktok.com/@Genevievejackbooks

x.com/genevieve_jack

MORE FROM GENEVIEVE JACK!

His Dark Charms Duet

Lucky Me

Lucky Us

The Treasure of Paragon

The Dragon of New Orleans, Book 1

Windy City Dragon, Book 2,

Manhattan Dragon, Book 3

The Dragon of Sedona, Book 4

The Dragon of Cecil Court, Book 5

Highland Dragon, Book 6

Hidden Dragon, Book 7

The Dragons of Paragon, Book 8

The Last Dragon, Book 9

The Angel of Paragon, Book 10

The Three Sisters Trilogy

The Tanglewood Witches

Tanglewood Magic

Tanglewood Legacy

Knight Games

The Ghost and The Graveyard, Book 1

Kick the Candle, Book 2

Queen of the Hill, Book 3

Mother May I, Book 4

Logan (companion novel)

The Wolves of Fireborn Pack Trilogy

Fated Bonds

Feral Instincts

Forever Mated

9 781940 675992